ATTACK
OF THE
INTERGALACTIC
SOUL HUNTERS

About the Author

Timothy Carter was born in England and raised in Canada. He currently lives and works in Toronto with his wife. He enjoys making people laugh, especially with his writing. He has been searching for spiritual truths since he was a teenager.

To Write to the Author

If you wish to contact the author or would like more information about this book, please write to the author in care of Llewellyn Worldwide and we will forward your request. Both the author and publisher appreciate hearing from you and learning of your enjoyment of this book and how it has helped you. Llewellyn Worldwide cannot guarantee that every letter written to the author can be answered, but all will be forwarded. Please write to:

Timothy Carter
℅ Llewellyn Worldwide
2143 Wooddale Drive, Dept. 0-7387-0847-X
Woodbury, MN 55125-2989, U.S.A.

Please enclose a self-addressed stamped envelope for reply, or $1.00 to cover costs. If outside U.S.A., enclose international postal reply coupon.

Many of Llewellyn's authors have websites with additional information and resources. For more information, please visit our website at
http://www.llewellyn.com

ATTACK
OF THE
INTERGALACTIC
SOUL HUNTERS

TIMOTHY CARTER

Llewellyn Publications
Woodbury, Minnesota

First Edition
First Printing, 2005

Cover art © © 2005 Mitch Hyatt / Koralik & Associates
Cover design by Gavin Dayton Duffy
Editing by Rhiannon Ross
Llewellyn is a registered trademark of Llewellyn Worldwide, Ltd.

Library of Congress Cataloging-in-Publication Data
Carter, Timothy, 1972-
    Attack of the Intergalactic Soul Hunters/Timothy Carter.
        p. cm.
        Summary: Ten-year-old Conrad, lover of science fiction, has dreams that feature him as a space adventurer named Hestar, but nothing has prepared him for the truth.
    IBSN 0-7387-0847-X (alk.paper)
    [1. Science fiction. 2. Extraterrestrial beings--Fiction. 3. Reincarnation--Fiction. 4. Psychics--Fiction] I. Title.

Llewellyn Worldwide does not participate in, endorse, or have any authority or responsibility concerning private business transactions between our authors and the public.

All mail addressed to the author is forwarded but the publisher cannot, unless specifically instructed by the author, give out an address or phone number.

Any Internet references contained in this work are current at publication time, but the publisher cannot guarantee that a specific location will continue to be maintained. Please refer to the publisher's website for links to authors' websites and other sources.

Llewellyn Publications
A Division of Llewellyn Worldwide, Ltd.
2143 Wooddale Drive, Dept. 0-7387-0847-X
Woodbury, MN 55125-2989, U.S.A.
www.llewellyn.com

Printed in the United States of America

Prologue

Conrad Viscous was having the dream again. It was his favorite dream. He had it three times a week at the very least, and it always blew him away.

This time there were asteroids. Sometimes there were alien bases, other times starship corridors, and even a few alien worlds. No matter the setting, it was always the same dream because he was only called Hestar in them.

Hestar was an alien, with reptilian skin, reptilian features, and backwards-bending knees. He rode some kind of spacebike, flying through an asteroid belt with a dozen or so aliens on similar bikes hot on his tail. He was always being chased or attacked in these dreams, which was fine with him. He always got away and he always won.

The chasing aliens fired a volley of lasers, which Hestar avoided by circling a large chunk of rock and using it as a shield. He spun around and doubled back, catching his pursuers by surprise and frying two as he flew through them.

"Hah, ha!" he cried. "Score two for the He-man."

The aliens gave chase again. Hestar saw their deadly beams of energy shoot past him and hit some more asteroids ahead. Debris blew off and flew at him, and Hestar had to fly frantically to avoid being pulverized.

"That was close," he said. "Time to fight dirty."

As Hestar flew through a cluster of small, spinning rocks, his left hand flicked a switch marked Homing Mines. Conrad knew, the way you instantly do in dreams, what they were: small, triangular-shaped explosive charges that homed in on enemy spacecraft.

Hestar made a sharp left and circled another asteroid, then stopped to check on his mines. The weapons had entered the small, spinning rock cluster, making them practically invisible to the enemy aliens. When the aliens tried to negotiate the cloud of rocks, the mines zoomed in and destroyed two of them. Another swerved to avoid a mine, struck a rock, then spun away out of control.

"Yeah!" Hestar said, but his cheer was short-lived. The rest of the mines hit the rocks and exploded harmlessly, and eight enemy aliens remained.

Hestar let off a battle cry and charged them again, firing all his weapons. The aliens were prepared this time, and they met Hestar's volley of lasers with their own. Hestar's spacebike took two hits as he closed the distance, and another as he sped past. The shots had been glancing blows, not enough to rupture his fuel cells and destroy him. They did, however, disable an engine and one of his forward guns.

With one engine down, Hestar could not escape them, and with one gun not functioning he could not fight them head-on. It was time for the weapon of last resort. Hestar reached down and thumped a button marked GravaCharge.

As before, Conrad had no idea what a GravaCharge was until that moment. Hestar clearly knew all about them, and seemed annoyed he had to waste one. Conrad knew then that they were an expensive item, and Hestar only had the one. If it didn't get those aliens off his back, he would be space debris.

Hestar looked over his shoulder as the charge fell away behind him. The aliens saw what it was, and they swerved to get away.

"Too late," Hestar called at them as the charge went off and became a miniature black hole. Everything in a radius of 100 yards, including all the remaining aliens, was sucked into the charge's singularity and crushed.

"Gotcha," Hestar said, turning back around.

A small asteroid chunk flew right at him. Hestar reacted on instinct, swerving to the left.

Not quite fast enough. The rock struck the side of his spacebike and sent it spinning, throwing Hestar off into space. The bike tossed end over end and smashed into another asteroid, exploding in a brilliant flash of light.

Hestar tumbled through the void at the mercy of the rocks. A large chunk flew past him, and its gravity well flung him in a new direction. If anything hit him, no matter how small, he would be dead.

Just then, a shape approached him. Conrad thought it was another rock, but it was a face. An alien face, old and wise-looking, with green skin and long, white hair. Conrad recognized it; he'd seen it before somewhere, but he could not think of where. He hadn't seen it in any of his previous dreams, but he knew the face just the same.

As it approached, the asteroid field disappeared. Conrad found himself in a soft-colored void, alone with the alien head.

"Hestar," the face said. "At last I've found you."

There was a blinding flash of light.

And Conrad sat bolt upright in bed.

"Whoa!" he said. "What was that all about?"

Chapter One

"I had the dream again," Conrad said as he took his usual seat at the front of the school bus the next morning.

"You did not," said Knowlton Cabbage, a dark-haired ten-year-old, as he took the seat beside him. "You're such a phony."

"I did!" Conrad said, pulling a toy helmet out of his schoolbag and putting it on his head. "And I would know. I was there."

"If you did," Knowlton put on his own plastic Police Force helmet, "you'd be in a good mood instead of your normal grumpy self. The dream always puts you in a good mood."

It was true, Conrad had to admit. Being an intergalactic hero for a night was an awesome thrill, and usually filled Conrad with excitement.

"Not today," Conrad said, wincing as the first ball of paper missed his helmet and bounced off his cheek. "It was weird this time. I died, I think. And there was this face."

"Was it the face of death?" Knowlton asked, looking over his shoulder to spot the thrower. Dean Trowler, a brute of a boy in a leather jacket, waved at him.

"How the heck should I know?" Conrad said, sinking lower in his seat. "It didn't look like anything I've ever seen before . . . wait," he paused. "I have seen that face before."

"You've seen the face of death?" Knowlton asked. "Was it scary and creepy and stuff?"

A ball of paper pinged off his helmet and landed in the aisle. Behind them, Dean snickered.

"No, not the face of death!" Conrad said, smacking his friend on the leg. "The face I saw, the alien face. I knew I'd seen it before."

"So you know an alien," Knowlton said. "Maybe you are an alien. Maybe he's your real father. It would explain a few things."

"Don't talk about my father, Knowlton."

"Know," Knowlton said. "Call me The Know."

Knowlton liked it when people called him Know, or The Know, which he encouraged them to do when talking about him. Conrad was the only person who made an effort, and when most people talked about Knowlton they used a different name. Several, in fact.

"I felt like I was going to die, and then I saw an alien face," Conrad said, pausing as an orange bounced off his helmet and landed on the seat behind him. "I don't know why I recognized it, but—"

"Take your orange back, loser," said one of the two boys sitting behind them, tossing the fruit over the seat back and into Knowlton's lap.

"You take it, one-cell," Knowlton shot back, tossing the orange over his shoulder at them.

"Hey!" snapped the bus driver. "No throwing stuff."

"They started it," Conrad said, pointing over his shoulder as an apple bonked him on the nose.

"I know what I saw," the driver said. In fact he had seen all the objects thrown at Conrad and The Know, but he didn't care about that. In his opinion, geeks deserved whatever they got.

"Sit still, an' don't go makin' noise," the driver said. "I mean it."

"Whatever," said Knowlton.

"And pick up all the trash when we get to the school," the driver added, sick monster that he was, knowing full well what would come next.

"Oh, help," Conrad said as everyone on the bus stood up and whipped paper balls, pens, rulers, lunch supplies, or anything else that was handy. The two ten-year-old boys ducked down in their seats and tried to shield themselves from the attack while the driver watched their plight in the rearview mirror. He laughed. The other kids laughed, and the barrage lasted all the way to school.

"Tomorrow," Conrad said, "we're gonna need umbrellas."

"I hear that," Knowlton agreed.

The bus pulled up beside the school, and the students started filing and pushing and shoving their way off. The driver waited until they were gone, then he turned to the first seat.

"Okay, you geeks, start cleaning up this . . . what the—?"

Conrad and The Know were long gone.

"That worked well, didn't it?" Knowlton said as he and his friend made their way through the crowd of students into the school.

"Brain over bus driver," Conrad said as he limped along behind him.

Conrad had a limp. No one knew why. His leg was fine; his family doctor hadn't found anything physically wrong with it. His parents had assumed it was a ploy to get attention, so they'd ignored it.

It wasn't a ploy. Conrad felt real pain in his leg. He just couldn't figure out why.

"It's as if we'd engaged stealth mode," Knowl-ton continued, walking slower than he could have so his friend could keep up. "Wouldn't you agree?"

"I would say," Conrad replied, "it was more like the stalking of Ninja Officer Bryne in Episode 37."

The school was L-shaped, dark-colored, and oppressive. The walls seemed to leer at them as they approached, and they always felt their mood drop when they entered its fluorescent-lit corridors.

"Why do you think that?" Knowlton asked as they walked down a crowded, noisy, and fluorescent-lit hallway to their homeroom. "In Episode 37, Ninja Officer Bryne was infiltrating the Xaxon Base, which was empty of all other beings at that time."

"Yes, but," Conrad said, "he had to evade the sensor drones in the walls, and he did it by using the Xaxon dancing plants for cover. By mimicking their movements—"

"Ah, yes, I see your point," Knowlton said. He actually thought his stealth mode description had been fine, but had learned from years of experience that some battles with his friend were just plain pointless. He also suspected his friend felt the same way about him.

"I'm glad that you do," Conrad said as they arrived at their first classroom of the day. "It is wise to bow to those with a higher capacity for intelligence."

"Then you should be bowing to me, you ugly pile of hamster poo," Knowlton said, taking his seat at the front of the class.

"No, you should be bowing to me, you mutant donkey stench," Conrad replied, taking the seat beside him.

"Either way," Knowlton said, "at least we don't have to clean up a pile of garbage that isn't ours."

At that moment, everyone else in the class stood up and pelted them with balls of paper and crumpled pieces of trash. Conrad and Knowlton flattened themselves against their desks, grateful that they had kept their helmets on.

A second or two after the barrage ended, the teacher walked in.

"Well, well, well. Looks like you boys have made quite a mess," he said. "Clean this up right now. And take off those stupid helmets. You look like a couple of geeks."

The class roared with laughter. Conrad and Knowlton sighed, then got down on their hands and knees and began cleaning.

Chapter Two

"Space," said Mr. Snouter, "as I'm sure you all know, is a very big place."

"The infinite beyond," Knowlton said, and a few students chuckled.

"Do you have something to add?" Mr. Snouter asked, turning to face him.

"I was just musing," Knowlton said, giving himself credit for using the word musing, "that space is infinite."

"He was saying the line from that stupid TV show," Dean Trowler said from his seat at the back of the class. Dean was the school's soccer and hockey hero, and held a special place in Mr. Snouter's heart.

"Ah," said Mr. Snouter. "And which television program would that be?"

"*Infinite Destiny*," said one of Dean's friends.

"Space, the infinite beyond," quoted Dean. "And infinite are the adventures of Captain Lassiter and his—"

"Yes, yes, I believe I understand." Mr. Snouter tapped his chalk against his impressive nose. "Funny man with large ears, correct?"

"Mr. Woaf," Knowlton said. "And those aren't his ears. It's an organic sensor array that—"

"Perhaps," Mr. Snouter said, "we could spend less time on televised fantasies and more time on the lesson?"

"Yes, Mr. Snouter," Conrad said, hoping his friend would take the hint and shut up.

Knowlton did keep silent, but Mr. Snouter wasn't about to let him off the hook so easily.

"You see, children," the teacher said, "the science of space observation and travel is very different from what you see on television. For example, spacecrafts do not hop from planet to planet in a matter of seconds or even a matter of days. The distances between planets and stars are far too great. Why, even a trip to the moon would take several days, and a rocket journey to Mars, our closest solar system neighbor, would take quite a few months. It simply isn't possible to fly through space to a distant galaxy and be back in time for tea."

The class laughed at this. Knowlton, however, did not.

"Not at our level of technology," he said.

Conrad groaned. Why did his friend have to make things worse?

"Did you say something?" Mr. Snouter rounded on him. "Would you like to share your thoughts with the whole class?"

"I was saying that kind of space travel isn't possible with our level of technology," Knowlton said. "But for a more advanced civilization—"

"Mr. Cabbage," the teacher said, "do you know what the speed of light is?"

"Twelve million miles per second," Knowlton said.

"Very good," Mr. Snouter said. "Do you know what the term 'light year' means?"

"The distance light can travel in a year," Knowlton replied.

"Tremendous," Mr. Snouter said. "Can anyone tell me how large our galaxy is?" He turned his attention on Conrad. "How about you, Mr. Viscous?"

"Um . . ." Conrad said.

Knowlton scribbled furiously in his notebook and held it for Conrad to see.

"A hundred thousand light years," Conrad read.

"Exactly," Mr. Snouter said, and he turned back to Knowlton. "Mr. Cabbage, let us suppose that your television spacecraft . . ."

"Starship Destiny," Knowlton said automatically.

". . . The Starship Destiny, then," Mr. Snouter said. "Let us suppose it is capable of travelling at the speed of light. How long would it take to cross the galaxy?"

"Well," Knowlton said, "if they engaged their spacewarp engines they could cross it in three hours."

"If they were travelling at maximum space-warp velocity," said Conrad, unable to help himself. "And they only use that for emergencies."

"But they could do it," Knowlton pointed out.

"But they don't have a space-warping thingie," Mr. Snouter said. "It doesn't exist. The fastest speed in our universe is the speed of light. At that speed, how long would it take your space craft?"

"Well, under those unimaginative limitations," Knowlton said, "it would take a hundred thousand years."

"Precisely," said Mr. Snouter. "One hundred thousand years to travel the length of one galaxy, let alone many galaxies or the depths of intergalactic space. And it is physically not possible for any man-made object to travel at that speed."

"But the technology of the twenty-fifth century," Knowlton said, "allows their starships to get around that issue by—"

"You can't get around reality!" Mr. Snouter snapped, finally losing some of his cool. "And reality is the world we live in, not some made-up television fantasy. There are no space ships, no ray guns, no galactic governments, no space-warp engines. Are we clear on that?"

"Of course," Conrad said. "We were just saying that—ow!" He rubbed his head where the rubber eraser had hit him.

"Good," Mr. Snouter said, winking at Dean before returning to the blackboard. "Who can tell me the names of the planets in our solar system?"

Knowlton raised his hand and a rubber eraser hit him, too.

When recess came, Conrad and Knowlton made a dash for the doors. If Dean and his gang of school bullies caught them, they'd spend the next fifteen minutes getting swirlies.

"Do you see him?" Conrad asked as he huffed and puffed, trying to keep up with his friend.

"He's not within sensor range," Knowlton replied, holding the door to the school grounds open for Conrad. "But he may be in stealth mode, or stalking like Ninja Officer Bryne in Episode 37."

"Then let's make warp for the tires," Conrad said.

The tires were three tractor tires that had been half-buried in the ground between the slides and the baseball diamond. Made from hard, black rubber, they were strong enough to stand on yet pliant enough for a child to squeeze into each side. The thick treads on their outer surface made them fun to climb, but the smooth, wide interior made them good hiding places.

"We made it," Knowlton said, stuffing himself inside the first tire.

"Of course we made it," Conrad replied, stuffing himself in opposite Knowlton. "We had a head start and have the advantage of brains."

"I do, anyway," Knowlton said.

"What?" Conrad said. The tires covered their heads, and the acoustics were all weird. Noises from outside the tire were reduced and concentrated into a background hum, making conversation a bit more of a challenge. It was like sitting inside a seashell and talking over the sound of the sea. The smell was weird, too. Like processed cheese mixed with tar.

"I said," Knowlton spoke up, "I have the advantage of brains, unlike you."

"Hey, I've got more brains than you, you Tallderian slugfish," Conrad said, relishing the chance to reference Episode 15.

"No, I'm definitely the smart one here," Knowlton replied. "And I can prove it, too."

"Oh yeah? How?"

"Because I'm the Know."

"That's not proof!"

"It's enough for me," Knowlton said. "And if you had the brains to realize it, it would be enough for you, too." He paused. "You Andromedan treeworm."

"You," Conrad pointed a finger, "had to think about that."

"At least I do think," Knowlton shot back.

And the bickering and episode-referencing continued for a further ten minutes.

"Okay, okay," Conrad said when he'd had enough. "I wanted to talk about my dream, not get into an argument with a primitive life form."

"Don't argue with yourself, then," Knowlton suggested. "Tell me about your dream."

In the last five minutes of recess, Conrad filled his friend in on the adventure he'd had as Hestar in the asteroid field.

"I still say Hestar is such a phony name," Knowlton said when Conrad had finished. "I mean, come on, who'd have a name like that for real?"

"I'm not making it up!" Conrad snapped. "This alien guy Gennex called me by that name three dreams ago, remember?"

"Oh yes," Knowlton said. "Gennex, that name sounds familiar. Isn't that the name of the Kathalan Ambassador from Episode 12?"

"That was Grenthrax," Conrad said. "Now come on, what do you think these dreams mean? Especially the last one with the face."

Knowlton thought about telling his friend he was suffering from brain damage, but decided against it. Conrad was clearly shaken by the last dream, so the time for jokes was over. Knowlton also realized his friend was relying on him for his superior knowledge and intellect, and about time, too. He couldn't help but feel flattered.

"It could be a message from outer space," Knowlton said. "Not unlike the telepathic message Roxwanna sent Captain Lassiter in Episode 2 and again in Episode 29."

"This is nothing like that!" Conrad said. "In Episode 2, Roxwanna used her telepathy to call for help, and it wasn't even the captain she contacted in Episode 29."

"I know, let me finish," Knowlton said. "What you've got is more than a short message. You're getting this Hestar guy's memories beamed into your head. For some reason, he wants you to know what he knows."

"But why?" Conrad asked.

Knowlton would have answered, but suddenly an impact on the tire above his head drove all words from his mind.

"Got 'em!" said a voice that could only have come from a jock. Legs swung down on either side of the tire, and the boys realized they'd been found.

"Hey, geeks!" called Dean as he and two other large boys approached. "What're ya eating under there?"

"We aren't eating anything," Conrad replied.

"I said," Dean crouched down beside the tire while his friend jumped off and blocked the other side, "what are ya eating under there?"

"Are we supposed to say underwear," Knowlton asked, "like we don't get it?

"If you don't," Dean said darkly, "you're gonna get it. What are you geeks doing in this stupid tire, anyway?"

"We wanted to talk to things more intelligent than you," Knowlton replied, picking up a pebble. "Hello, stone. How are you?"

"Knowlton . . . " Conrad hissed. Getting beaten up was not high on his list of favorite things.

"You losers think you're so smart, don't you?" Dean said. "Well, think your way out of this!"

Two bicycle chains came into view, and before Conrad or Knowlton could react, the chains were swung around them. The bullies yanked the chains tight around the tire and locked them, trapping the two boys inside.

And then the school bell rang.

"Let's go, guys," Dean said, winking at the boys in the tire. "Wouldn't want to be late for class."

"Yeah, see ya later, losers," said one of the others, and the three bullies walked back to the school.

Chapter Three

"Well," said Knowlton. "We're in a bit of a pickle."

"No, we're in a tire," Conrad said, waving his left arm frantically.

"Why are you waving your left arm frantically?" Knowlton wanted to know.

"So that someone at the school will see us and come and help," Conrad replied.

Knowlton raised an eyebrow at him. Conrad hated it when his friend did that. It meant Knowlton was about to call him stupid.

"You're stupid," Knowlton said. "So what if someone sees us? They won't help. They never do."

"A teacher might see," Conrad said.

"Like the teacher who saw Dean and his buddies giving us swirlies?" Knowlton pointed out. "Or the one who watched us get shoved in the mud after he'd insisted we try out for the football team?"

"Okay, fine, so we won't get help," Conrad said. "Do you have any bright suggestions?"

"We could try and push these chains up and over our heads," Knowlton suggested.

They gave it a go. The chains were tight, locked around their arms at the elbow, making even the smallest squirm a tremendous effort. Behind them, the chains were caught in the tire treads, making their progress virtually impossible.

"This is impossible!" Conrad said after half an hour of squeezing, pushing, and grunting. "We're stuck here."

"Nothing is impossible," Knowlton said. "Remember when Lassiter and Argis were chained to the pole and sentenced to die in Episode 62? They got out of that one."

"Yeah, because Argis used the reflective surface of his communicator badge to deflect the laser that was going to kill him," Conrad replied. "The laser cut the chains and they were free. We don't have lasers and we don't have comm badges."

"But we could do something similar with what we do have," Knowlton said. "Do you have your reading glasses on you?"

Conrad reached up and patted the pocket where he kept his glasses. He hated them, but he needed them for reading textbooks and doing school work. Bullies called him "nerd" and "four-eyes" when he wore them, so he kept them tucked away in his pocket until they were absolutely necessary.

"Yeah, I got them," Conrad replied.

"You could use them to focus the sun's rays onto the chains," Knowlton said, "just like they did with the ship's main reflective saucer in Episode 21."

"That's stupid!" Conrad said. "The sun won't burn through these chains."

"No, you're right," Knowlton said. "But it could probably burn the rubber of this tire."

"Yeah, but we're in the tire."

"It would give us a good reason to get out of it."

"Aarg!" Conrad cried. "Are you just trying to mess with my head?"

"Yes," Knowlton said. "We clearly won't get out of this by ourselves, so I thought I'd keep your mind busy for a while."

"You little . . . " Conrad said, struggling for the right insult as his hands strained forward for Knowlton's neck.

Knowlton, well out of his friend's reach, watched with amusement.

"If I had a Syledi sabre gauntlet, I could finish you off," Conrad said. "Then I'd slash through these chains like this."

As he said it, his right hand made a slashing movement.

As he did it, a beam of pure white energy extended from his hand, slicing through the chain binding Knowlton. It flashed off as quickly as it had come, but an afterimage burned in both boys' eyes.

Conrad and Knowlton sat still for a while, not saying anything, their mouths open in astonishment. Finally, Knowlton cleared his throat and spoke.

"That was kind of cool," he said. "Do it again."

Far out in the cosmos, billions of light years away, something registered. A spike of a very specific type of energy was detected, and traced to Earth.

A being followed the trace to its source, moving at the speed of thought, traversing the intergalactic and then interstellar distances in a matter of seconds.

He had found him. After eleven years of searching, Cyscope had finally found him.

Chapter Four

"How . . . " Conrad said. "The heck . . . " he added. "Did I do that?"

"How should I know?" Knowlton said, peeling himself out of the tire. "Ahh, that feels better."

"Hello?" Conrad said. "I'm still stuck in here."

"So do that laser hand thingie and cut your own chain," Knowlton said, squatting beside the tire and picking his chain up. "Look at that. You really did cut right through it."

"But how?" Conrad said.

"I'll say it again," Knowlton said. "How should I know? Maybe you have super powers or something."

"Be serious!"

"I am," Knowlton said. "How else would you explain it?"

"I don't know," Conrad said. "And how come you're so calm about all this?"

"Would it help if I freaked out?"

"No," Conrad said. "Well, it might make me feel better."

"Too bad," Knowlton said. "Look, I'd better go get the principal to cut you loose. That is, unless you can do that laser thing again?"

"I'll try," Conrad said. He lashed out with his right arm, and Knowlton leapt up onto the tire.

"Ow!" Conrad said as his friend's weight hit his head. "Did I do it?"

"I don't know," Knowlton replied. "I was too busy getting out of range."

"What?"

"Well, I don't want to get cut in half."

"Okay, stay up there," Conrad said. "I'm going to try again."

He tried again. His hand swept out, but nothing happened.

"Nothing happened," Knowlton told him. "Maybe there's a trick to it, like what that Tree-manian witch did with her hands before she could fire a mystic bolt. You remember?"

"Episode 11," Conrad said. "So what should I do with my hands?"

"What were you doing with them before?"

"I don't remember," Conrad said, giving it another try. Still nothing.

"Okay, I'll go get help," Knowlton said. "You keep trying."

Knowlton hopped down on the other side of the tire and headed off to the school building. When he was out of sight, Conrad turned back to the chain that bound him.

"Okay, let's see what we can do," he said, whipping out his hand again and trying to make it happen. It didn't, and after several tries he got bored.

"Why isn't it working?" he asked his hand, giving it a serious looking at. "Maybe I have to hold my fingers in a special way. Or maybe I push something."

Conrad held his fingers in all kinds of different positions, then he tried pushing his thumb onto imaginary buttons on his palm. Then he tried holding his thumb in weird positions while pushing buttons with his fingers. Nothing.

Conrad sighed and sank back into the tire. It had been a fluke, a one-time thing. There was nothing to do but sit there and wait for Knowlton to get back with help. And maybe catch a quick nap.

Conrad closed his eyes and waited for rescue, and started to doze. A few minutes later he fell asleep, and dreamed of a long corridor.

Having arrived in spirit on the world called Earth, Cyscope searched for a suitable host body. He could not affect the physical plane unless he inhabited a body, and becoming a newborn would leave him helpless and without memory for years. That left one option—possession.

Cyscope flew through the city, invisible and unheard, looking for a native who was open to being taken over. There were always several to choose from on any world, and in no time at all, he found one.

The man was short, fat, and very miserable. He stood on the concrete railing of a bridge that spanned a valley. He was planning to jump. That much was clear from the mental and emotional signals Cyscope had picked up on and followed. Miserable people bent on self-destruction left themselves wide open to possession.

Cyscope descended on the man like a hawk attacking its prey, slamming into his body and forcing the man's soul out. The body shuddered, convulsed, and nearly fell over the side, but Cyscope took control and balanced just in time.

He turned and hopped down from the railing. Cyscope tested his new body, raising and dropping the arms, flexing the fingers, jumping on the spot. A few cars slowed down as they passed him, their drivers curious, but Cyscope paid them no mind. He needed to find out his new body's strengths and weaknesses, and acclimatize himself to this brave new world.

He began walking, heading in the direction of the energy signature he'd picked up in deep space. Behind him, the soul of the body he'd stolen drifted away on the wind.

Ah, thought Conrad. *It's the corridor dream again.* When he'd had this specific dream before, he had led an attack on this place. Aliens had leapt out of doorways on either side of the corridor, firing beams from ray guns. Their aim had been poor, and Hestar had taken all of them out.

This time was different, however. The corridor looked a little different, and he was aware that his hands were bound. He looked right and left and saw he was being led down the corridor by two alien guards. Mostly humanoid, the guards had eel-like hair and strong, two-fingered hands.

They came to a room at the end of the corridor. When Hestar looked over his shoulder past the guards, Conrad realized why it had looked different. In every other dream, he'd been charging the other way down the corridor, away from the room he was now being pushed into.

Two guards stood inside the room in front of a really nasty-looking alien. Thick, purple-skinned muscles bulged under a black uniform, and the antler-like bone structure sprouting from his head resembled a crown. A full head taller than Hestar and the two guards, he seemed to project power and terror from his alien pores. Conrad had never seen him before, and yet he recognized him instantly.

"Hestar, how good of you to join us," said the nasty-looking alien. He stood before a large, round screen built into the floor, which projected an image of several galaxies in the air.

"Cut the small talk, Cyscope," Hestar said. "What do you want with me?"

"You found something that doesn't belong to you," Cyscope said. "Emperor Kubris wants it back. Where have you hidden it?"

Cyscope stood to one side, and gestured at the holographic galaxies.

"Where have I hidden what?" Hestar said, but Conrad could tell he knew exactly what the alien was after. Something very important. Something of such monumental significance that it could not only tip the balance of power in the galaxy, it would shatter it altogether.

The dream blurred and refocused. Hestar was looking down at the floor, drips of blood falling from his face. He was in pain, and his bound arms were still held tightly by the guards.

"I don't understand why you continue to resist," Cyscope said, and a rough hand grabbed Hestar's head and jerked it up. "After all, you have nothing to gain by your silence." Cyscope's fingers felt smooth yet sharp, like the skin of a shark.

"You going to talk me to death?" Hestar said, his voice slurred.

"If you talk," Cyscope went on, "you will be rewarded. Paid for your information, just like always. So why do you resist?"

Before Hestar could answer, the floor screen exploded upward and a large, stocky robot with jets in his feet smashed through. Clinging to its metal shoulders was another alien, one whom Hestar knew very well. Long-eared and duck-billed, he looked like a rabbit crossed with a platypus.

"Gennex!" Hestar cried to his maroon-skinned friend. "It's about time."

A light sword appeared in Cyscope's hand, but Gennex shot him in the shoulder. Cyscope fell back, then turned and ran for the far door. The robot grabbed the guards holding Hestar, and slammed them together with bone-crunching force.

"Opposition defeated," said the robot.

"Great work, Tink," Hestar said, pulling weapons from the guards' belts. "Let's get out of here."

"Right behind you, good buddy," Gennex said, taking a second weapon for himself.

Hestar opened the door and stormed down the corridor, shooting at alien guards as they popped out of the doorways on either side. This is more like it, Conrad thought. This is the dream I remember.

But just as it was becoming very familiar, everything froze. As it did, a face appeared before him, the same face he'd seen at the end of his dream the previous night.

"Hello, Hestar," the face said.

"Who are you?" Conrad asked, aware that it was he who was asking now, not Hestar. "What's going on?"

"You are in danger," the face said. "He has come."

"He?" Conrad asked. "Who?" Even as he asked, an image of the alien, Cyscope, flashed through his mind.

"You must act soon, Hestar," the face said. "You have been found."

"Found? What?" Conrad asked, feeling the dream slipping away all around him.

"The soul holds the key," the face said as it disappeared. "The soul holds all the answers."

The dream ended with a flash of light, and Conrad was back in the tire. The chain still held him, and there was no blade of light projecting from his hand.

He heard footsteps approaching, and he looked outside the tire to see Knowlton returning with Mr. Thurman, the school principal. The tall, bald man carried a large pair of bolt cutters, much to Conrad's relief.

"So, got yourself into some trouble, have you?" Mr. Thurman said, kneeling beside the tire. "I imagine you've skipped a few classes, too."

"That's hardly fair, sir," Knowlton said. "Like I told you several times, we were chained

and unable to move. If my chain hadn't broken
. . ."

"Ah, yes," Mr. Thurman said, cutting through
the chain binding Conrad. "I remember. Your
chain suddenly broke, just like magic."

"It did," Conrad said, pulling himself from
the tire. "I saw it."

"Uh huh," said the principal. "Let me tell
you what I think happened. You boys were
playing a little tie-up game, then you decided
to cut a few classes."

"No, sir!" Conrad said.

"It's not like that at all," Knowlton added.

"You both have detention," the principal
said. "I'll see you after school. Now, back to
your classes."

Principal Thurman marched the boys back
to the school building, then left them in the
stairwell that led up to the second floor. They
were currently missing English class, and they
hurried along the hallway to the classroom.

"I can't believe he didn't believe us," Conrad said.

"Oh, he believed us," Knowlton replied as they reached the classroom door. "He just doesn't like us."

"Him and everyone else," Conrad said. "Why is that?"

Chapter Five

Cyscope stood on the corner of Yonge and Bloor, one of Toronto's busiest intersections. People moved all around him, hurrying to lunches and meetings and appointments, but all of them swerved to avoid the alien in his new human skin. It wasn't a conscious choice on their part; they simply sensed something different about him that made them nervous.

Cyscope couldn't have cared less about their concerns. He was on the hunt. Somewhere in this city was the soul he was looking for, and he would find him.

He stretched out with his senses, feeling the spirits of those around him on the corner, then stretching out further and further. He knew from his stolen body's memories that the people on this planet had not developed their psychic abilities to any significant degree. Few, if any, would be aware of his probe.

Cyscope's quarry was another story, however. As soon as he found a soul that matched the pattern he was looking for, Cyscope knew he would have to move quickly.

After a minute of searching, Cyscope found a pattern that matched. He kept searching, spreading his senses to their widest circumference, and found a few more. In total, he counted seven souls who vibrated with the right kind of energy. Now it was simply a matter of checking them out, one by one.

Cyscope focused his senses on the closest matching spirit and started walking.

After walking for ten minutes, he got bored and took the subway instead.

Conrad and Knowlton kept their plastic helmets on as they left the school bus that afternoon. They knew they weren't safe from attack until they were a good ten yards away.

Strangely enough, it had been their detention that had spared them from their usual bus-ride barrage. They had missed the regular school bus because of the punishment, and had to take the detention bus instead. The only people who took the detention bus were kids who stayed late for sports or school plays, and those who actually had detention. There were only nine people on the bus that night, and they soon ran out of things to throw.

"Another day done," Knowlton said as he removed his helmet.

"Sure is," Conrad agreed, taking off his own. "Want to come over for a bit? Watch some *Destiny*?"

"That would be a great plan," Knowlton said, "but I suspect our late arrival back in the neighborhood has not gone unnoticed by our parents. I'd better report home before I consider other options."

"I copy that," Conrad said. He'd already told his friend all about his second dream, and about the warning the alien face had given him. He wanted to discuss it some more, maybe ponder who the face had said was after him, but it was not to be.

Knowlton was right; they had to face their parents.

"Conrad, out," said Conrad, touching his wrist where an imaginary communicator, or comm, was strapped.

"Knowlton, otherwise known as The Know, out," said Knowlton, touching a similarly imagined comm. "Good day, my friend."

"Fare thee well," Conrad said, and they parted ways.

Knowlton headed off for his house one street over. Conrad had been over a few times; his parents were pretty weird, but the place was nice. *A lot nicer than my place*, he thought. Probably because Knowlton's parents had jobs.

Conrad hobbled over to his home, the last house on the block. It was a small, one-level place, with cracked, peeling paint and a front porch that was a tangled booby trap of death. Conrad picked his usual safe path over the rotted boards, unlocked the front door, and went in.

"You're late," his mother said.

"I had detention," Conrad replied, taking off his coat and dropping it on the floor.

"What'd you do this time?" his mother asked.

Conrad turned to look at his mother. She sat hunched over on a cheap plastic chair in the living room, wearing the same tank top and shorts she'd worn for the last three days. Her hair was stringy and unkempt, her posture was bad, and she was starting to smell. A small cloud of cigarette smoke hung in the air above her.

She sat facing away from him at a rickety wooden table, playing games on her computer. The carpet beneath her was dirty and stained. It was home to an unspeakable number of creepy-crawlies. The walls were ugly and bare, and the couch was ratty, torn, and smelled vaguely of fish.

Yet, the television, VCR, and DVD player were brand new. So was the stereo equipment beside it. And even though the table looked like it would fall apart at any second, the computer system in front of Conrad's mother was the very latest model.

"I didn't do anything," Conrad said. "As usual. Is that a new computer?"

"Daddy's check came today," his mother said. "I had just enough for the down payment."

"Oh," Conrad said, wincing at the mention of his father. The divorce had ended a year ago, and boy had it been messy. At the time, Conrad had worried they'd end up on one of those daytime talkshows. Conrad's mother won everything, including custody of Conrad and a monthly alimony check.

"Is it a good system?" he asked, watching his mother play computer solitaire. It was all she had ever done with the last one, even though it had been capable of so much more. Conrad had used it to look at *Infinite Destiny* websites and to email fans around the world, but his mother only wanted the solitaire.

"Well, it cost a lot of money," his mom replied.

"Oh," Conrad said. "Can I have the old one?"

"Nope," his mom said. "I sold it to Sheryl, three doors down. Got four hundred bucks off her."

"That's great, Mom," Conrad said. "I'll be in my room. Later."

"Later," his mom said.

Her eyes never left the screen.

Conrad's room was the entire basement, give or take a few cardboard boxes filled with old and useless odds and ends. His bed was in the corner farthest from the furnace and laundry room, and was nothing more than a cheap box spring and mattress set.

He had a chest of drawers for his clothes, toys, and comic books, but of course he hardly ever used it. His mom complained about the mess sometimes, but not often. If she did, he would point out her own lack of cleanliness, and what could she say to that?

Conrad stepped over some toys, nearly slipped on a comic book, and sat down on his bed. He had nothing to do until suppertime, if his mom remembered about dinner, so he decided to watch some *Infinite Destiny*.

Conrad selected a cassette, then popped it into his very own VCR. It used to be the family VCR, as had the television above it. The first thing his mother had done with her first alimony check was to buy a new TV and VCR set. Having no use for the old ones, she gave them to Conrad. It was the one thing Conrad got out of the divorce. His father got even less, which was more than he deserved.

Conrad settled down to watch. Completely by accident, Conrad had chosen the first episode he'd ever seen, the one his father had been watching when he'd walked in the room six years ago.

Conrad remembered the event almost as well as the episode in question. His father had been flicking channels, and only watched a minute's worth before deciding the show was garbage. He'd been about to change channels again, but Conrad, utterly mesmerized, had begged him to leave it on. In a rare act of generosity, his father had relented to Conrad's pleading.

Conrad had watched the show ever since, using his allowance to buy cassettes to tape it.

When his father and mother fought, he'd watch a taped show to tune them out, and to escape.

Conrad watched, fast-forwarding through the opening credits and commercials and getting to the meat of the story. Captain Lassiter's father, a humble tradesman like Conrad's own father, was visiting his son's ship for a routine trade show. The two had grown apart; the father hadn't wanted his son to enter the Space-Fleet, and they hadn't talked since. By the end of the episode, however, the father told Captain Lassiter how proud he was of his son's accomplishments.

When he'd seen that episode, Conrad saw his own father in a new light. Maybe someday, he'd thought, my dad will say he's proud of me. Conrad had doubled his efforts at school, hoping to earn that praise.

All that ended during the first and only custody hearing. Conrad's father hadn't even tried, ending the meeting with a curt, "You can keep the little geek."

Conrad picked up his pillow and threw it at the TV. When that failed to have an effect, he thumped the eject button and threw the tape across the room. It made a satisfying crash as it shattered against the wall.

He regretted it immediately; he liked that episode, and there were lots of other shows on that tape. Still, the loss wasn't huge. He could always get those episodes from Knowlton.

"Hey!" his mother snapped. "What're you doing down there?"

"Nothing," Conrad said, looking at the mess he'd made. "Nothing at all."

Cyscope watched the house, sensing the people inside. There were two people, one male and one female, and the male vibrated with the right frequency. If that was his quarry, his mission was almost over.

He walked up the steps to the house and rang the bell.

Chapter Six

To Cyscope's disappointment, the female answered the door. If it had been the male, he would have known if it was his quarry right away.

"Can I help you?" the female asked, her voice fearful. "This really isn't a good time, we're about to have dinner."

"I must speak with the male in your household," Cyscope said.

"The . . . what?" the woman answered. "Look, I'm really sorry, but you'll have to leave."

Cyscope studied her. There wasn't much to see; she stood hunched behind the door, ready to push it shut at a moment's notice. Cyscope wasn't used to this planet's physical forms, but he could tell she was very uncomfortable. She was shorter than he was, and likely felt threatened by his presence.

It was to be expected. Her soul sensed the difference in vibration between them, and that which was different was frightening. Cyscope didn't have the patience to try and put her at her ease. Drastic steps would have to be taken.

In one swift motion he slammed both hands against the door, snapping it backward into the female and knocking her cold. Cyscope stepped over her unconscious form and went inside.

His arms hurt. Cyscope realized his current body was not accustomed to exerting such force. He would have to be careful of that in the future.

The male came in from another room, and took in the scene with shock. He was bigger than Cyscope, much more of a threat than the woman. The situation had caught him off his guard, however, and he hesitated. Cyscope ignored the pain in his arms and moved, grabbing the man and pinning him to the wall. Then, holding him firmly, Cyscope stared into his eyes.

It is often said that the eyes are windows to the soul. As Cyscope stared into the man's eyes he saw into his soul, and knew right away he was not his quarry. Cyscope, and those with similar abilities and discipline, could probe the soul's memories of past lives. Some beings could block vital information from such a probe, but none could hide their identities.

The male's current name was John Menzies. He had indeed come from Cyscope's galaxy, and was a soldier for the Deltran Empire in his past life. He had met his previous life's end during a battle with the Light Movement, the largest organized rebellion in that corner of the universe. His soul had drifted through the cosmos to this galaxy, and had been reincarnated here thirty years ago.

"Admiral Cyscope?" John said. The probe often unlocked past-life memories in the one being probed, and sometimes the flow of information went both ways. The man had known Cyscope, or knew of him. And, he had been a loyal soldier.

"Hello, John Menzies," Cyscope said, "You could be useful to me."

Conrad and his mother ate cold spaghetti for the third time that week. They could have had hot spaghetti—the microwave was brand new, and in perfect working order—but Mrs. Viscous simply didn't care enough to heat the leftovers up. And if she didn't care, Conrad thought, why should I?

He also didn't care enough to start a conversation. If he did, he knew where it would go. He'd ask all the questions, and she'd reply with one-word answers.

"How was your day?"

"Fine."

"Anything interesting happen?"

"No."

"Did you do anything?"

"Solitaire."

"Anything exciting in the mail?"

"No."

"Do you want to hear about my day?"

"No."

That was how it would go. So what was the use?

However, Conrad realized there was one question that had been bothering him ever since he'd destroyed his *Infinite Destiny* tape. Luckily, it was a question to which a one-word answer would be preferable.

"Mom?" Conrad asked. "If Dad had wanted custody, would you have fought him for me?"

His mother raised her head and gave him a don't-be-so-stupid look.

"Of course, dear," she replied.

Wow, Conrad thought, his eyes bulging in surprise. He'd expected her to say no, but instead she'd given him a three-word yes!

"Really?" he said, all smiles.

"You bet," she replied. "I get much better alimony money if I have a kid."

"Oh," Conrad said, his spirits dropping back down again.

"Ah, don't sweat it," his mom said. "You're a good kid, Conny."

"Whatever," Conrad said, and was silent for the rest of the meal.

That night, Conrad dreamed. It wasn't one he recognized, but it was cool.

He was Hestar, and he was in some kind of alien training zone. All around him, aliens were working out. Some lifted weights, some ran on a track, and some climbed vines into the huge trees that fenced the training zone.

Hestar sat on a flat, soft surface that reminded Conrad of the mats they used in gym class. He sat in a circle of aliens, one of whom was the same wise, old alien from his last two dreams.

He was more than just a floating head this time; he had an alien body that was not all that different from Hestar's own. He was reptilian, just like Hestar, but he had white hair sprouting from his head and chest. And, his knees bent forwards. Conrad knew right away that he was the teacher, and all the other aliens were his students.

The wise, old alien pointed to two aliens in the circle. The first was large and strong, and even hairier than his teacher. In fact, he looked like a walking carpet. The second alien was tall and thin, and looked like he was made of matchsticks. The two aliens stood, bowed to each other, and fought. To Conrad's amazement, swords of light blazed from their hands.

Just like the thing that came out of my hand, he thought.

The aliens dueled around the inside of the circle. After a couple of fierce clashes, the hairy alien drove the thin one out of the circle. They bowed, and the thin one sat down.

It's a sword-fighting class, Conrad realized. *Super cool!*

The wise, old alien pointed to a short, stocky alien with blue skin. That alien stood, bowed to the hairy alien, and extended his own light sword. They fought, but all too soon the hairy alien shoved the shorter one out of the ring.

Man, Conrad thought. *That hairy guy's pretty good. But I bet I could take him.*

And then, the wise, old alien pointed at him.

Uh oh, Conrad thought, but Hestar didn't hesitate. He leapt into the circle, not bothering to bow before attacking his opponent.

The hairy alien was caught off guard, and Hestar drove him back. Conrad was amazed at how well he was doing; Hestar really knew how to handle a light sword.

"Soulblade," a voice said, cutting into the dream. "It is called a soulblade." Conrad recognized the voice—it was the wise, old alien again.

Not now, Conrad thought. *I'm kicking that guy's—*

"Aarg!" the hairy alien cried as he tripped backwards over a sitting alien and fell out of the circle. Hestar strode around the mat, his arms raised in triumph, and Conrad couldn't help but feel a little smug.

"Remember how to use it," the voice said. The dream froze and faded, and the wise alien head appeared once more. "You will need it soon."

"What?" Conrad asked. "Why?" He could feel himself waking up, and he struggled to stay in the dream long enough to get some answers.

"He is coming," the voice said. "Be ready."

And then the dream ended.

Chapter Seven

"Any new dreams I should know about?" Knowlton asked, adjusting his helmet as Conrad approached the bus stop.

"I saw the face again," Conrad replied, putting on his own helmet as he arrived at the street corner. "Twice, actually. He told me someone is looking for me, and that I've got to remember how to use my soulblade."

"What," asked Knowlton, "is a soulblade?"

"Remember that light sword that came out of my hand?" Conrad said. "That's a soulblade."

"Oh," Knowlton said. "Cool. So, did he say anything else?"

"No, that was pretty much it," Conrad said. "How'd things go with your parents yesterday?"

"Don't ask," Knowlton said.

"Why do we have such rotten parents?" Conrad asked.

"Why do we have such rotten lives?" Knowlton said. "Oh, look, here comes the bus."

"Do you think the driver has forgiven us for yesterday?" Conrad asked.

The bus approached their corner without slowing down. The driver made an obscene gesture as he drove past, and the kids on board pelted the two boys with eggs and tomatoes.

"It would seem not," Knowlton replied, wiping some yolk from his face.

"Looks like we're walking today," Conrad said. "Or we could ask our parents for a ride."

They paused. Then they burst out laughing.

"Walking it is," Knowlton said.

And walk they did. It was a long way to school, at least an hour or so by foot, but what else could they do?

"We could just go home," Conrad pointed out.

"You could," Knowlton sighed. "Your mom wouldn't care. But my parental units are not so forgiving of such things. Already I am grounded a week for getting detention. After we're late today it will only get worse."

Conrad nodded, silently agreeing. He'd met Knowlton's parents a few times, but once had been more than enough.

He decided to change the subject.

"Who is the better captain?" he said.

"Oh, not this again . . . " Knowlton sighed.

"Come on, which captain is better?" Conrad said. "I still say it's Captain Lassiter."

"You are so uninformed," Knowlton said, as Conrad knew he would. "If you take all possible factors into account, you can only conclude that the best is Captain Frederik Wong from *Infinite Destiny: The New Fate.*"

"You're such a traitor," Conrad said. "Any true fan would say that the original captain was the greatest."

"Captain Wong has all the benefits of both the Chinese and Russian culture," Knowlton pointed out.

"Captain Lassiter," Conrad said, "has hair."

And so their arguments went for the next half hour as they walked onward to the school. It was slow going with Conrad's limp, but they kept their chins up and their spirits high.

Soon it began to rain, and they both got soaked.

Cyscope sat at John Menzies's kitchen table, clad in a pair of plaid cotton pajamas. He was barely awake; this species, it seemed, needed more time to get themselves together after a period of rest. Or perhaps it was just this body he'd chosen. Whatever it was, it was taking all of Cyscope's considerable spiritual training to bring his mind back into focus.

"Here, sir," John said, entering the kitchen with a steaming cup of hot liquid. "Drink this. It will make you feel better."

Cyscope accepted the cup and swallowed its contents. The fluid was very hot, and it burned his tongue and throat.

"Eagh," he said, throwing the cup at his subordinate. "What was that filth?"

"Coffee, sir," John said. "And you are supposed to sip it slowly."

"Warn me next time," Cyscope said. "And bring me some food. I have much to do today."

John hurried off to make breakfast. Cyscope watched him go, eyeing him with contempt. This John would be of limited help at best. As Cyscope recalled, he hadn't been that great of a warrior during his past life. He couldn't produce a soulblade, and knew only basic hand-to-hand combat.

Plus, he'd put up such a fuss when they'd tied up his wife the night before. Cyscope had explained that, having had no previous incarnation in the Deltran Empire, she would only get in their way.

John hadn't liked it, but he'd agreed for Cyscope's sake. His loyalty was without question, and his house would serve as an adequate base of operations. Now, if he could only prove himself an adequate cook.

"Try these, sir," John said, setting a plate down in front of his master. On the plate were two thin, brown pastries, smelling vaguely of strawberries. "They are called Pop Tarts. Enjoy."

When he'd finished eating, Cyscope moved to the living room to meditate. His mind felt clearer, less groggy—perhaps there was something to this coffee, after all. He settled down in the middle of the carpeted floor, just in front of John's bound and gagged wife. She sat silently in her chair, having given up struggling long ago.

Cyscope reached out with his senses, and immediately detected the presence of two alien souls. They were close, and they were heading his way.

Without hesitating, Cyscope leapt to his feet and rushed for the door.

"Is it much farther?" Conrad asked, wearing his jacket up over his head to keep the rain off him. It helped a little, but not much.

"You know as well as I do we have five more blocks to go," Knowlton said, letting the rain drench him. "Hey, look at that guy."

Conrad looked. A short, balding man with a big tummy was walking along the sidewalk towards them. He had no umbrella, which wasn't particularly strange. The downpour had come suddenly, after all. It wasn't all that strange that he was barefoot, either. It was autumn, but not that cold out yet.

It was odd, however, to go out dressed in one's pajamas. The man wore plaid cotton pajamas, which clung to his body as the rain soaked them through. The man seemed unconcerned by this, and when he looked up and saw the two boys, he walked faster.

"What is his problem?" Conrad asked, but he had a powerful desire not to find out. There was something about the man that bothered him, something that had nothing to do with his taste in outdoor clothing.

"Maybe we should—" Knowlton began, taking a step back.

Run! cried a voice in Conrad's head, echoing in every corner of his mind. In fact, it seemed to speak directly into his soul.

"Let's move," he said, grabbing Knowlton's arm and turning him around. "Go!"

They took off, Knowlton sprinting and Conrad hobbling for all he was worth.

Behind them, the man broke into a run.

Cyscope pumped his body's arms and legs, making it move as fast as it was able. The two kids must have recognized him, and he could not let them escape. If one of them was his quarry . . .

The night garments he wore felt cold and heavy, and Cyscope wished he had taken the time to change into more appropriate clothing. Soon, however, such petty things would no longer concern him. He was gaining on the children, and one of them appeared to have a bad leg.

Bad leg . . . yes. That made sense.

Cyscope caught up to the limping child and grabbed him, yanking him off his feet.

"Hey!" Conrad cried as he was pulled backward into the crazy man's grasp.

The man spun him around, clasped both his wrists in one hand and held them down. With his other hand, he grabbed Conrad by the chin and forced him to look into his eyes.

"What do you want?" Conrad began to say, but his words trailed off as his mind was filled with images. Many of them he recognized from his dreams, but many were new. They felt like the memories of someone else. This someone was not a nice person, either.

"Stop it!" he cried as he saw visions of killings and torture. "Stop it, Cyscope . . . "

Conrad had no idea how he knew the man's name. It had simply popped into his head, and he knew.

"You remember me," the man said. "Just as I remember you, Hestar."

Conrad gasped. How could this man know the name from his dreams? He must be connected somehow. Maybe the dreams weren't dreams at all. Indeed, that wise, old alien head had told him someone had found him. He thought it was all very cool, but at the same time he'd been sure they were just dreams.

But this was no dream. This was really happening. And, whoever this Cyscope was, he was bigger and stronger and knew a lot more about what was going on than Conrad did.

"You," Cyscope said, tightening his grip, "are coming with me."

"I think not!" Knowlton shouted, swinging himself around a lamp post like a superhero and kicking Cyscope in the face.

Cyscope let go of Conrad and staggered back, stunned. Knowlton grabbed the back of his friend's jacket and tried to pull him away.

"Come on, Conrad," Knowlton said. "We . . . " he stopped, looking at Conrad's arm.

The soulblade was back, gleaming from the end of Conrad's hand. Raindrops sizzled into steam when they touched it, making a loud hissing sound.

"What?" Conrad asked, his mind still a mess. He turned to face his friend, and the light beam sliced through the lamp post.

Cyscope recovered his senses and lunged for the kids. As he did so, the lamp post fell into him and knocked him into the street.

"Whoa!" Knowlton said, backing off.

"Whoa," Conrad said, holding up his hand and looking at the glowing soulblade.

"Whoa!" cried Cyscope as a truck swerved to avoid the fallen lamp post and slammed into him with a sickening crunch.

"Holy . . . " Conrad said, his hand falling to his side, the soulblade vanishing. He stared at Cyscope's body lying in the street, and couldn't think.

"Yikes," Knowlton said. "Is that guy dead?"

"Nnn . . ." was all Conrad managed to say.

"Yuck," Knowlton said. "Just like Episode 12."

Conrad considered that for a moment. Then he turned and ran.

"Hey, wait up!" Knowlton called, running after him.

They went two blocks before Conrad stopped suddenly. Knowlton caught up, and Conrad looked over his shoulder at him.

"I think," he said, "you mean Episode 13."

Then he was off again. Knowlton followed, struggling to keep up. He couldn't understand why his friend was outrunning him, and then he realized something.

Conrad was no longer limping.

"Weird," Knowlton said, keeping his friend in sight.

Chapter Eight

Cyscope hovered over the accident scene, recovering from the sudden shock of death. It was always a shock for Cyscope, though other beings described it as peaceful.

The body he'd been using lay still in the middle of the road, the rain streaming down his expressionless face. A crowd was gathering rapidly, and the driver of the truck was trying desperately to revive him. Cyscope knew the struggle was useless; if the body could have been salvaged, his spirit would not have been expelled.

Cyscope allowed himself a moment of anger. He had been careless, his quarry had escaped, and his body had been destroyed. He would need to possess a new one before he could continue the chase.

Hestar was more dangerous than he'd anticipated. Cyscope had expected him to have no memories from his previous life, yet clearly he knew enough to summon his soulblade on command. With time he would remember even more, and would become a formidable adversary.

And who was that boy with him? His spirit was not of this world, either. Could it be Hestar's companion, Gennex?

Cyscope realized he'd need help, more than his newly awakened soldier, John, could provide. He would need his elite tracking team, the Hunters.

Cyscope sped off through the cosmos, toward Deltran Prime.

Conrad sat, his eyes fixed straight ahead. He'd taken refuge from the rain out of habit, even though he'd hardly noticed the downpour. His mind reeled from what had just happened, both inside and out.

He'd just seen a man die. That was pretty horrible, especially since he'd had more than a little to do with it. It was so different, watching it for real. It wasn't like TV at all.

But there was something more disturbing going on in his head. For a moment there, when his light sword—soulblade—had come out, he'd felt something come over him that he didn't like. It had been as if someone had tried to take over his mind.

Conrad wasn't sure he believed all that stuff Cyscope had been saying, but if it was true and he had been Hestar . . .

Was it possible for a past life to take over your current one? Or was he still Hestar, but he hadn't quite remembered yet? Did the fact that he was Conrad Viscous even matter?

Who was he?

Knowlton found Conrad under a train bridge. His friend sat up near the bridge's underside, hugging his knees and staring at nothing. A freight train was rattling by overhead, and under the bridge the noise was tremendous. Knowlton, who stood down by the sidewalk, had to cover his ears. Conrad didn't seem to notice at all.

"Con," Knowlton called, shouting to be heard over the train. He climbed up the embankment to where his friend sat. The closer he got, the louder the train noise was, and he wasn't sure he could stand it. Fortunately the last car soon passed, and the two boys were left in relative silence.

"Conrad?" Knowlton said, waving a hand in front of his friend's face. "Am I going to have to do the Maldoran Thought Grip on you?"

Conrad said nothing, so Knowlton grabbed his friend's head and dug his fingers into the scalp.

"My thoughts grip your thoughts," he said, quoting the words of Psychic Officer Lysta. "Show me what you are thinking."

"Ow!" Conrad yelped, swatting away Knowlton's hand. "That hurt."

"I sense you are in pain," Knowlton said. "And you are having an emotional buildup."

"Stop talking like Lysta," Conrad said, rubbing his head. "You're not a Maldoran. That stuff's not real. But my dreams are."

"What, you mean those space dreams?" Knowlton said.

"Of course those dreams!" Conrad replied. "What other dreams would I be talking about?"

"But how can they be real?" Knowlton asked.

"Maybe they aren't really dreams," Conrad said. "Maybe they're memories, but from a past life."

"Okay, this is getting freaky," Knowlton said. "I mean, Lysta talks about her past lives on *Destiny*, and I think it's her spirit in Galen's body in *The New Fate*. But, Con, that's just a show."

"I know," Conrad said. "But what's happening to me . . . that guy! The guy who grabbed me. He called me Hestar. And then you kicked him, which was really cool, by the way."

"Thank you."

"But then there was this," Conrad said, holding up his right hand. A beam of energy sprang forth from it, extending to a yards away from his fingertips. "I know this is a soulblade.

I know how to call it up. Normal people can't do that."

"Yeah, good point," Knowlton said, staring at the glowing blade. "And that was pretty cool, the way you cut that pole in half and knocked the weird dude into the path of that—"

"Don't remind me!" Conrad said. "I mean . . . I killed him."

"Yeah, he's a real pavement pastry."

"Knowlton!" Conrad said. "That's really gross. That guy was a person, and now he's—"

"Roadkill," Knowlton said. "Hey, I'm sorry, but it wasn't your fault. He attacked you, and you defended yourself."

"I guess," Conrad said. "But still, a guy's dead, Knowlton. That's just . . . "

Conrad thought long and hard for words that would express just what a man's death was. It had shaken him like nothing else he'd experienced in his life.

"Look," he said at last, "I've got to find out if this stuff is really true." He stood up, and started down the slope.

"How do we do that?" Knowlton asked as he followed Conrad down the slope to the sidewalk.

"We talk to someone who knows about past lives," Conrad replied. "We have to find a psychic."

"Velcome to de parlor of Madame Cecillia," said the woman in the large and pouffy hat. "Twenty dollars for a crystal ball reading, thirty for a message from de spirit vorld."

Conrad and Knowlton looked up at her, then at each other.

"Fake," they said together, and they turned and left the parlor.

"This is a big waste of time," Conrad said as they walked away from Madame Cecillia's Psychic Parlor. The sun hadn't come out yet, but the rain had stopped an hour ago.

"I disagree," said Knowlton, scanning the page they'd torn from a phone book. "So far we've had excellent luck in finding all the fake psychics."

"True," Conrad said. "And we're getting better at spotting them. They all wear big, pouffy hats."

"And they talk like vampires," Knowlton added. "You know, vould you vike to vuck an egg?"

"Yeah, exactly," Conrad replied, and they both laughed. "But, useful though it is to find all the fakes, where are we going to find a real psychic?"

"Maybe a real one will find you."

The two boys spun around and saw a teenage girl standing behind them. She was tall and thin, with purple-dyed hair and tattoos up and down both her arms.

"You just came to see my mom, didn't you?" the girl said. "Don't worry about the whole Madame Psychic act, she does that because it's what most people expect."

"So under the silly hat, she's a real psychic?" Knowlton asked.

"No," the girl said. "But I am. She does the act, I give the readings. It works out. And pays for my tattoos. So, you boys need some help?"

"You could say that," Conrad said.

"She just did," Knowlton pointed out, and Conrad punched him in the arm.

"Would it have something to do with the fact that your souls are from another galaxy?" she asked.

"Whoa!" Conrad said. "How could you possibly know that?"

"I told you," she smiled. "I'm a psychic."

"In that case," Conrad said, "we need your help."

"Come with me," the girl said. "Say, what are your names?"

"I'm Conrad, he's Knowlton," Conrad said as they walked back to the parlor.

"Call me The Know," Knowlton said.

"Aren't you going to ask me my name?" the girl asked.

"We figured it would come up in conversation," Knowlton said.

"What is your name?" Conrad asked.

"Debbie," she replied as they reached the parlor. "Debbie Vadaro. But don't call me that. I only answer to Lysta."

Conrad's eyes bugged out and so did Knowlton's.

"You mean . . ." Conrad began.

". . . Like the psychic officer . . . " Knowlton added.

". . . on *Infinite Destiny*?" Conrad finished.

"Yeah, that one," Lysta said. "You guys are fans?"

"We're total Desties," Conrad said. "Wow, you're a teenage girl and you like *Destiny*. That's so cool."

"Thanks," Lysta said, and she let them into the parlor.

"Velcome to de parlor of . . . oh, it's you kids again," said Madame Cecillia.

"Hi," said Knowlton while Lysta closed the door behind them. "Is Cecillia your real name?"

"I told them, Mom," Lysta said. "I'm going to give them a reading on the house."

"On the house?" Lysta's mom said, looking at the two boys. "Well, they do look poor. All right then. But come back if a paying customer comes."

"Sure," her daughter said. "This way, guys."

The two boys followed her around back, then up a flight of stairs that led to the apartments above the boutique. To the left was a well-cleaned kitchen, a far cry from the mess Conrad's mother kept. To the right was a short hallway that led to a bathroom, a closet, and two bedrooms. Lysta led them to her room and opened the door.

"Wow," said Knowlton, as his and Conrad's eyes went wide. "You really are a Destie."

The room was small, messy, and wallpapered with *Infinite Destiny* posters and cutouts. There were shelves stocked with novels based on the show, biographies of the actors, and episode guides. Her dresser was covered in action figures and spaceship toys. The boys even noticed that, among the many articles of clothing on the floor, there were several *Infinite Destiny*-themed T-shirts and shorts.

"Knowlton, my friend," Conrad said, "we have surely found paradise."

"Come in and sit down," Lysta said, hopping up on her bed and gesturing for the boys to do the same. She didn't have *Destiny* sheets, Conrad noticed, but she did have themed pillowcases.

"Cool, aren't they?" Lysta said, grabbing one and stuffing it in her lap. "So, why don't you tell me what's going on? Why do you want a reading?"

"I want to know who I am," Conrad said.

"And to find out why that fat guy was after him," Knowlton added.

"A fat guy attacked you?" Lysta asked.

"You mean you don't know?" Knowlton said. "I thought you were a psychic."

"Yeah, you knew I was from another galaxy," Conrad added.

"I can read what's in the forefront of your mind when I get up close," Lysta said. "You were projecting that out-of-galaxy stuff loud and clear for anyone to see. For deeper information, I need to do more work. I need to sit you down and get inside your head."

"Ah," the boys said.

"Right now I'm getting an image of the fat guy," Lysta went on. "You know him," she pointed at Conrad, "and you," she pointed at Knowlton, "did some karate kick on his head. Not bad."

"Yeah," Conrad agreed, patting his friend's shoulder. "That was really cool."

"And then . . ." Lysta said, and stopped. "What the—holy cow, he's dead!"

"Yeah, total pavement pastry," Knowlton said.

"It was an accident!" Conrad pointed out.

"Yes, I'm seeing that now," Lysta said. "It's just . . . eeg."

"Tell me about it," Conrad said.

"And what's the deal with that light sword in your hand?" Lysta asked.

"It's a soulblade," Knowlton said. "At least, that's what the guy in his dream called it."

"It's a long story," Conrad added, seeing the puzzled look on Lysta's face.

"Tell me," Lysta said. "Then I'll be able to help you."

Five souls arrived in the city of Toronto. One was Cyscope, the rest were his Hunters.

They spread out, seeking bodies to inhabit. It didn't take them long. It never did.

When they had acclimatized themselves to their new physical forms, they began walking.

The hunt was on.

Chapter Nine

"It must be a universal constant," Knowlton said, taking a bite of his sandwich. "You can't beat peanut butter and jam."

Conrad would have said he agreed, but his mouth was full of the same thing. Instead he nodded and gave the thumbs up.

They had told Lysta everything that had happened, from Conrad's dream up to the fight with Cyscope. By that time it was early afternoon, and the boys were very hungry. Lysta went to help her mother do some readings, leaving them to eat their bagged lunches in the kitchen.

"Hey, Know," Conrad said when he swallowed, "you remember that flying kick you did? How did you do that?"

"Sometimes I surprise even myself," Knowlton replied.

"No, seriously," Conrad said. "How did you do that?"

Before he could answer, Lysta came back up the stairs and joined them.

"Woo," she said, taking a can of pop from the fridge. "Some people have too many problems. Makes my head hurt."

"Does that mean you can't read me?" Conrad asked.

"Oh, no. Just give me a few minutes," Lysta said.

"It's like the Lysta in *Destiny*," Knowlton said to his friend. "She would always get these pains if she used her power too much. And there would always be a shot from her point of view where everything's green and swinging back and forth."

"This isn't as bad as that," Lysta said. "Ten minutes and I'll be fine."

The boys finished their lunches while Lysta sipped at her drink. They talked about *Infinite Destiny* and why it was so cool, and occasionally talked about other stuff.

"My mom didn't want me to drop out of school," Lysta said, "but when Dad died we were pretty hard up for cash. The psychic parlor was my idea. We set it up, but then I had to stay home and work."

"Well, you're not missing much," Conrad said. "For us, going to school means being constantly surrounded by people who want to beat us up."

"Yeah, and teachers and bus drivers who turn a blind eye," Knowlton added.

"Really?" Lysta said. "I went through something like that, too. It's to be expected when you have an alien soul."

"Huh?" the boys said.

"You have alien souls," Lysta told them.

"I know," Conrad said.

"I do?" Knowlton asked.

"I could sense you were both different," Lysta said. "Other people can sense it, too. They just don't realize it. People can be very afraid of things they don't understand."

"I see," Conrad said. "That explains a bit."

"I'm an alien, too?" Knowlton said.

"Yes," Lysta said. "Don't worry about it, so am I. Lots of people are, actually. Souls travel all over the universe in between lives. It's kind of neat, if you think about it."

"Yeah, cool," Knowlton said, and he smiled. "Wicked! I'll bet I'm an intergalactic bounty hunter, like Remmix from Episodes 39, 51 and 60.

"But wait a second," he added, having a thought. "Why haven't I been having dreams with cool space battles like Conrad?"

"That's what we're going to find out," Lysta said. She finished her drink, scrunched up the can, and tossed it into the blue box by the fridge. "I have an idea, though. Conrad, I think that someone is trying to contact you."

"Who?" Conrad asked.

"Someone from the spirit world," Lysta said. "Most likely someone you knew in your past life."

"Maybe that weird alien head from his dreams?" Knowlton suggested.

"Hey, yeah!" Conrad said. "I'll bet it is."

"Give me your hands," Lysta said, reaching hers across the table. "Let's see what we can see."

Across the street, a Hunter stopped and turned to look at Madame Cecillia's Psychic Parlor. He smiled.

He'd found him.

Quaz, the Hunter, crossed the street. There weren't too many cars about, but one skidded to a halt and honked its horn at him. Quaz ignored it.

He pushed open the door to Madame Cecillia's and went in.

Lysta shuddered, her breath caught in her throat. Her eyes bulged wide with terror as she tried to speak but couldn't.

"She's choking!" Conrad said, trying to free himself from Lysta's hands.

"I don't think so," Knowlton said as he watched.

Lysta looked down at the table. When she looked up again her eyes looked different, half asleep yet deadly serious. She started to speak in a language neither boy understood, but before they could comment her words seemed to flow into English. If either boy had commented, they would have said her translator was faulty.

"Hestar . . . " Lysta said. "Hestar, they are coming . . . you must escape . . . "

"Who are you?" Conrad asked.

"No time . . . must escape . . . " Lysta said. "Already here . . . "

"Who?" Conrad asked.

Lysta's eyes widened, and she gripped Conrad even harder.

"Quaz is here!" she screamed at him.

There was a scream from downstairs. Conrad and Knowlton turned to look at the stairwell door, and they heard footsteps stomping up towards them.

"Go!" said the being inside Lysta. Then she was released. She jerked back so quickly her chair fell over.

Knowlton ran to the door and locked it.

"You okay, Lysta?" Conrad asked, rushing to help her.

"Ow," she said, taking his hand and waiting for him to pull her up. "That really hurt my head. Pull me up, okay?"

"Oh, sure," Conrad said, and he helped her to her feet. "What happened to you?"

Before she could answer, there was a rattle on the doorknob, followed by a loud slam.

"Somebody wants in," Knowlton said, retreating to the kitchen. He flung open the closet and pulled out a mop, and held it like a weapon.

"Going to clean him to death?" Conrad asked.

"Omigod!" Lysta cried. "Mom!"

And then, something punched through the door. It was long and bright, and when Conrad saw it he knew right away it was a soulblade. With a few cuts the door was gone, and the doorway was on fire.

A man stepped into the apartment. He looked to be in his early twenties, with a shaved head and a jean jacket over his strong shoulders. The soulblade blazed from his right hand.

"Hestar," the man said. "I am Quaz. Come with me now, and your friends will be spared."

Chapter Ten

Cyscope's new body was much older than the last one, and had many more limitations. Clearly a homeless person, the body was dirty, smelly, and hairy all over. He wore a ratty, knee-length coat over torn, uncomfortable clothes.

But that wasn't the worst of it. The man had also been a heavy drinker. Indeed, his state of extreme drunkenness had left him wide open to possession. Cyscope had had to deal with many of the aftereffects of being in such a state when he'd taken over the body.

He had not been alone in this, either. Two of his Hunters, Eelt and Vellen, had taken control of two other intoxicated people, presumably the first drunkard's friends. They too had suffered for their bodies' condition, and Eelt had thrown up. It had not been pleasant at all.

However, they had been trained to deal with much worse, and they were professionals. They focused their minds on the task at hand, and set off in search of Hestar.

"Quaz has found him," Cyscope told the others, and they walked faster. "His soulblade is drawn."

Finding Hestar was not an issue. Cyscope knew exactly which soul he was looking for this time, and had imprinted that soul pattern on his Hunters. It was simply a matter of where they chose their bodies, and how quickly they could get to their quarry's location.

"Hestar is drawing his own blade," said Eelt.

"He wants to fight," said Vellen.

"We must hurry," Cyscope said. "Zepher and Vorla will meet us at Hestar's location. Remember, I want him immobilized, not killed. Is that understood?"

"Yes, Admiral Cyscope," Eelt said.

"Spoil my fun," said Vellen.

Conrad stared at the man who stood before him, and tried to think of what to do. If he didn't go with the man, he would kill Knowlton and Lysta, and maybe even Lysta's mom. But if he did go with him . . .

Conrad didn't know what would happen if he went with him, but he knew it wouldn't be good.

He also knew that he'd raised his right arm, and his own soulblade had extended. He hadn't consciously done so, and he wondered if Hestar was trying to take control again.

"So be it," the alien-possessed man said. "I'll start with your friend, here."

"I don't think so," Knowlton said, swinging the mop.

"I do," Quaz said, dodging the mop and then slicing it with his soulblade.

Conrad was already moving. As Quaz reared his arm back for a death blow, Conrad leapt in front of his friend and deflected Quaz's blade with his own.

He had no idea how he did it. His body simply reacted to the situation. Even his limp had been forgotten.

"Get away from my friends, slimeball," he said, slicing his soulblade around in an arc that cut through Quaz's shirt.

Quaz roared in rage and lunged at Conrad, his soulblade thrust out like a spear. Conrad swung away from the potential stab and sliced again, this time cutting Quaz's shoulder. Quaz yelped in surprise and pain, then swung clumsily. Conrad blocked, then attacked with his own blade.

They dueled. Conrad fought with a skill he didn't know he had, easily deflecting the alien's blows and forcing him back along the corridor toward the bathroom. There was genuine fear on Quaz's face. He clearly hadn't been expecting much of a fight.

"Way to go, Conrad!" Knowlton cried, cheering his friend on. "Go get him! Chop his head off!"

Panic suddenly filled Conrad. He seemed to be winning the fight, but what was he supposed to do to finish it? Kill Quaz? Conrad didn't think he could. The accidental death of Cyscope that morning had been too much for him. Cold-blooded murder was out of the question.

Wound him, then? Sure, but how? Cut off a hand or a foot? But then he might bleed to death. If only he could knock him out somehow . . .

The alien entered the bathroom and Conrad followed, keeping up his attack while pondering his problem. Even if he did knock the man out, he would only come after him again when he woke up. Somehow he'd tracked him, though Conrad had no idea how.

He had to kill him. But he couldn't do it.

The alien tripped on the door of an open cupboard below the sink. He fell into the space between the toilet and the bathtub, his soul-blade vanishing as he landed. He was stuck, but Conrad knew it wouldn't last very long.

This was his chance.

"Leave me alone," he said, and slammed the bathroom door closed.

"Did you get him?" Knowlton asked as Conrad rushed past him.

"We have to get out of here," Conrad said, taking his friend by the arm. "Now."

Flames spread from the burning doorway along the corridor. It occurred to Conrad, even as he and Knowlton dashed down the stairs, that the man in the bathroom might be in real danger.

There was no time to think about that now. They ran through the parlor and out the front door, where Lysta was dragging her semi-conscious mother onto the sidewalk. Madame Cecillia looked stunned, but was otherwise unharmed.

"Are you okay?" Lysta asked when she saw them.

"Well, we're not burned or anything," Knowlton said. "And Conrad was awesome! You should've seen him going at that guy—"

"What do you mean, you're not burned?" Lysta said. "Are you saying—"

"Your place is on fire," Conrad said. "But we can't worry about that now."

"A fire?" said Lysta's mom, waking up in a hurry. "In our home?"

"Forget about that!" Conrad said, looking back into the storefront for a sign of Quaz. "We have bigger problems."

"Indeed you do."

Conrad, Knowlton, Lysta, and Madame Cecillia spun around. There were three old men standing in the street behind them, all with soulblades drawn. Behind them, two teenage girls in private-school uniforms approached. They joined ranks with the old men, lighting their own soulblades.

"Who are you people?" Conrad asked.

"These are my Hunters," the lead old man said. "You already know who I am."

Conrad looked into the eyes of the leader, and knew in his gut that he was the same man who had attacked him earlier that day.

"Cyscope," he said.

"Correct," the alien in the drunk man's body replied. "Come with me now, Hestar, or I will show you pain."

Chapter Eleven

Conrad knew he was trapped. Ahead of him were five alien-possessed people, led by a being who had tortured him in a previous life. Behind him, fire spread through the storefront of Madame Cecillia's.

Conrad took a quick look over his shoulder into the shop, hoping to see a back door they could all make a run for. He didn't see one, but he did see Quaz, the sixth alien-possessed person. He looked burned and unhappy, and Conrad did not think they could all get past him before the other five aliens attacked.

It was an impossible situation. And it only got worse when Knowlton threw the beer bottle.

"I'll show you pain," Knowlton said, picking up a bottle from the street and hurling it at one of the old men. It struck Eelt square in his head, and he crumpled to the pavement.

"Whoa," said Knowlton, looking from his hand to the man's unconscious form.

"Wow," said Lysta, open-mouthed in shock.

"You choose the way of pain," Cyscope said. "So be it. Hunters, bring Hestar to me. Kill the rest."

Zepher and Vorla, the two teenage schoolgirls, darted forward. Vellen, the other old man, followed slowly, ready to be a second wave of attack should the girls fail. Quaz advanced on Knowlton, his blade held out lance-like before him.

"Now you've done it," Conrad said.

"What do we do?" Lysta cried.

"You're the psychic," Knowlton said. "You tell us."

"Now you all just stop this at once!" Lysta's mother screamed.

Conrad looked around. The situation, to put it mildly, was desperate. To put it bluntly, they were screwed. It was like that time Captain Lassiter was surrounded by Khorgs in Episode 26.

How did he get out of that one, exactly? Oh, yes. A miraculous rescue. Mr. Smirt, the engineer, turned up in a shuttle and whisked the captain away. It seemed unlikely to Conrad that the same luck would befall him.

Just then, a red sportscar screamed to a halt in front of him. The door flew open, nearly taking off his nose, and a voice from inside the car said, "Get in."

Before Conrad could do or say anything, a hand shot out, grabbed his arm, and yanked him into the car. A second later, the car sped away.

"What?" Cyscope shouted, clearly as surprised as the rest of them. "Bring him back here!"

Zepher and Vorla started to give chase, but Cyscope stopped them.

"We cannot catch that vehicle," he said. "Never fear. We will find him again."

"And these ones?" Quaz asked, pointing his soulblade at Knowlton, Lysta, and her mom. "You still want them dead?"

"No, not yet," Cyscope decided. "They may be valuable as hostages. Bring them."

"Hostages?" said Lysta's mom. "What is the meaning of this?"

Knowlton didn't wait for explanations. He grabbed Lysta's arm and pulled her with him, ducking around Quaz and taking off down the street.

"Run!" he called over his shoulder, hoping Lysta's mom would take the hint.

She didn't. She stood there like a true grownup, not believing that the situation was really happening. In a moment, Cyscope and Vellen had her.

"Mom!" Lysta cried, turning around.

"We can't stop," Knowlton shouted, pulling her along behind him. The two schoolgirls were giving chase, and Knowlton did not like the idea of being captured.

They were close to the Christie subway station. Knowlton led Lysta inside, and he leapt over the barrier and ran down the stairs.

"Hey!" the ticket collector roared as Lysta followed Knowlton's example.

The ticket collector rushed from his booth in time to intercept Zepher and Vorla. He grabbed them by the backs of their purple school blazers before they could leap the barrier.

"Oh, no you don't!" the collector said. "You're in big trouble."

Vorla ignited her soulblade and waved it in his face.

"Or not," he squeaked, letting them go.

Knowlton and Lysta reached the bottom of the stairs. There were stairs on either side of them that led down to the platforms, one for eastbound trains and one for westbound. Knowlton heard the sound of a train coming into the station, perfect for their escape. But which way was it heading?

He had a 50/50 chance, like Captain Wong had in Episode 14 of *The New Fate,* when he'd been locked in the Bylanian dungeon. Which way had he gone? And which way, Knowlton asked himself, should we go?

It was time to make a choice. Luckily for Knowlton, Lysta made it for him.

"This way," Lysta said, tugging him behind her to the stairs down to the westbound track.

Her guess was right. The train was there, but its door chimes were chiming. Knowlton and Lysta sprinted forward and just managed to leap aboard before the doors closed.

As the train pulled out of the station, Knowlton saw the two girls arrive on the platform. They in turn saw him, and they shouted and waved their soulblades. Knowlton gave them a wave before his car entered the tunnel.

"We got away," he said.

"But what about my mom?" Lysta asked. "And Conrad? Who was that guy who grabbed him?"

Knowlton had no answer for that. He watched the subway tunnel flashing past, and hoped his friend was safe.

"You are safe," said the stranger in the car. "At least for the time being."

Conrad looked up at the man who'd grabbed him. He was a well-built man in his late twenties, with messy, unwashed hair and a scraggly beard. He wore a business suit, complete with a tacky, striped tie, and his navy blue blazer was old and worn. Whoever he was, he sure didn't care much for appearances.

"Who are you?" Conrad asked. "Hey, we have to go back. My friends—"

"No," said the man. "I'm not here for them."

"What?" Conrad said, falling over in his seat as the car hung a hard left. They were driving at multiples of the posted speed limit and still accelerating. "My friends are in trouble! That old guy, I think he's Cyscope, said he was going to kill them."

"Not my problem," the man said.

"But—"

"Shut it, kid," said the man. "My job is to keep you out of Cyscope's hands until Pakfrida gets here."

"Pakfrida?" Conrad said. "Who's that? And for that matter, you never told me who you are."

"I'm Javix," the man said. "I'm a bounty hunter. Pakfrida is the guy who hired me."

"You're an alien?" Conrad said. "You don't look like one."

"Neither do you," Javix said.

"So you were born here, like me?" Conrad asked.

"No," Javix said. "I traveled here in spirit and possessed this human's body."

"You did?" said Conrad. "Why didn't you come here in a spaceship, or—"

"Because that would have taken too long," Javix snapped. "For a situation like this, spirit travel is much faster. No more questions, kid. Not until we're out of the city."

"Where are we going?" Conrad asked.

"What did I just say?"

"Sorry, but—"

"No buts. Shut it. Or I'll shut it for you."

Conrad shut it. They drove east along highway 401, leaving the city, and soon even the suburbs, behind.

"Home sweet home," Knowlton said as he and Lysta stood in the driveway in front of his house. It was a nice, two-level house, painted in light shades of beige and brown, virtually identical to every other house on the block.

Knowlton hated it. He found Conrad's house to be much more exciting. Lysta hated it as well; she hated beige.

"Well, let's go," Lysta said, walking to the front door. "We have to call the cops and tell them what happened to my mom and Conrad. You coming?" she asked when she saw that Knowlton was still standing on the driveway.

"Yeah, sure," Knowlton said. "Just . . . psyching myself up. Okay, I'm ready. Let's do this."

"You . . . okay?" Lysta asked as he opened the door. "I mean, I know it's been a weird day, but you seem kinda freaked out about something. Is it Conrad?"

"No," Knowlton said, hanging his coat up. "I'm sure he's fine. And I'm sure your mom is fine."

"Then what . . . ?" Lysta began, but before she could finish, a tall, fat woman stepped into view.

"Knowlton," said the tall, fat woman. "Where have you been?"

"I—" Knowlton began.

"Don't you interrupt when your mother is talking!" snapped Knowlton's dad, storming into view behind his mother. At least, he tried to storm. He was a thin man and he was short, a full head shorter than his wife, so he didn't have much weight to storm with. It was more of a pitter-patter, really.

"Your father and I are not pleased with you," Knowlton's mother went on. "Why weren't you in school? And who is this person?"

"She's—"

"Don't interrupt your mother!" Knowlton's father said.

"Tell her to leave," his mother said. "We have to have a talk."

"But—"

"Do as your mother says!" his dad snapped.

"Lysta," Knowlton said, "you're going to have to go."

"But Knowlton—" Lysta began.

"You heard him, young lady," Knowlton's dad said.

"But we have to call the police," Lysta said. "My mother has been kidnapped."

"What?" Knowlton's mom said, her anger gone in an instant. "Well, come in, come in! Knowlton, why didn't you tell us? This way, the phone's over here, you poor dear. What a frightening day you must have had!"

Knowlton's parents hurried Lysta to the phone. Knowlton stayed by the front door, shaking a little, his heartbeat slowly returning to normal.

Chapter Twelve

Conrad watched the landscape flashing past, and reflected that he'd never been outside the city before.

He also reflected on the fact that he was very scared and not at all comfortable with the man who had "rescued" him.

"Can I talk now?" Conrad asked.

"No," said Javix.

They sat in silence for a few more moments.

"Can I turn on the radio, at least?" Conrad asked.

"What's a radio?" Javix asked, his head tilting slightly to one side.

"Well," said Conrad, "it's a—"

"Never mind, I've got it," Javix said. "A communication device that picks up broadcasts, used to entertain and inform."

"Yeah, that's it," Conrad said. "Can I listen to it?"

"No," Javix said.

They rode in silence for a few moments more.

"How come you didn't know what a radio was one second," Conrad asked, "but you did the next, after your head did that tilt thing?"

"If I explain, will you stop asking me questions?" Javix said.

"Sure, I guess," Conrad replied.

"It's like this," Javix said. "When you possess a body, you take over completely and the soul that used to inhabit it is gone. You can access their memories and learn about things you need to know, like how to drive a car or what a radio is. It's like looking at files on a computer; you have to sort through them to find the stuff you want. So that's what I was doing just now, looking through the memories of the guy who used to live in this body for data on radios. Got it?"

"I guess so," Conrad replied. "Who was he, the guy you possessed?"

"Just some guy," Javix said. "He's not important."

"But—"

"We had a deal, kid."

"Sorry," Conrad said, turning away and leaning against the car door. He wished he had a pillow to put his head on. The fighting had tired him out, and he wanted a nap.

Conrad made himself as comfortable as possible, and after twenty minutes or so he managed to drift off.

He was back in the asteroid field, the same one from his dream two nights ago. It was like the sequel to that dream, the next episode. "Where we last left Hestar," a TV announcer might have said, "he was tumbling helplessly through a void of fast-moving rocks, whose very touch meant death."

But then . . .

Hestar saw something rocketing toward him. It wasn't a rock, but it was too small to be a ship. Another spacebike, maybe?

When it got closer, Conrad recognized it from other dreams. It was a robot, the same robot that had smashed up through the floor with Gennex in his last dream.

"Tink!" Hestar cried. "What took you so long?"

"I had to avoid your gravity charge," the robot replied over the comm. "Come with me."

"I have a choice?" Hestar laughed as the robot took hold of him and jetted them out of the asteroid field.

In the distance Hestar could see a ship, one which he knew well. Conrad knew it, too, from a dozen other dreams. It was a house-sized, arrow-shaped eyesore, a patched-together, Frankenstein's monster of a vessel, made from bits and pieces of every kind of space-faring craft and quite a few other things.

It looked like a pile of junk, but it was Hestar's pride and joy.

"The Magnus," he said. "My pride and joy. Daddy's home!"

"Looks like Tink's saved your sorry behind again," came Gennex's voice over the comm.

"Let's just get out of here," Hestar said. "I led those Trankans away from you, saving your own sorry behind."

A door on the side of the Magnus opened, and Hestar and Tink climbed inside.

The dream changed. Hestar and Gennex charged across a rocky plain, chased by a team of ant-like aliens with ray guns. They dropped down into a ravine and hid behind a boulder, then caught their breath.

"Six of them, two of us," Hestar said.

"And they have weapons," Gennex added. "We don't."

"Hardly seems fair," Hestar said.

"Yeah," Gennex agreed. "For them."

They listened as the aliens dropped down into the ravine and approached the boulder. Hestar and Gennex climbed up onto the rock and leapt down at them, screaming a battle cry. Before the aliens could react, the two friends were upon them, kicking and punching until all six were down.

"That was easy!" Gennex laughed, collecting up the aliens' weapons. "We rule the universe, by far."

"By far," Hestar agreed, pulling a blue gemstone from a pouch slung over his shoulder. "Sorry, boys," he tossed the gem in the air and caught it, "but this is mine now, and I don't feel like sharing."

Conrad, who had been enjoying the dream immensely, suddenly became confused. *Had Hestar stolen the gem? Were those ant guys simply trying to get it back?*

The dream changed again.

Hestar sat in a room full of robed people, each of whom had an arm outstretched. Some of them had soulblades glowing from their hands. Most did not.

Conrad understood that he was in a class, just like the one from his dream the previous night. No doubt this was the place where Hestar had learned to create his own soulblade. A figure stepped into view.

"Hestar, there you are," said the wise, old alien from Conrad's last several dreams. "Any luck yet?"

"No," Hestar replied. "This is a waste of time."

"Is it?" the alien asked, smiling a grandfatherly smile. "I wouldn't have given you this chance if I hadn't been certain you had the potential."

"Give me a break, Pakfrida," Hestar said, and then Conrad knew the alien's name. In fact he realized he'd always known it, he'd just forgotten.

"Just keep trying," Pakfrida said as he walked away. "And believe."

"That was a long time ago," the same voice said from behind Conrad, and the dream changed again. This time there was nothing but inky blackness, and Conrad was not Hestar but himself.

"Who are you?" Conrad asked, turning around and coming face to face with the disembodied head of the wise, old alien once more. "Okay, I know your name is Pakfrida, but . . . "

"You are safe for the time being," Pakfrida said. "Javix will protect you until I arrive to take you off-planet."

The face was fading, and Conrad could feel himself slipping away. He was starting to wake up. He struggled to hold on for just one more question.

"When will you get here?" Conrad asked.

"Five standard hours from now," Pakfrida said, just as the dream ended.

Conrad woke up just as the car left the 401. Javix pulled the car into a gas station, then did his memory search. Then they waited.

"Shouldn't someone be coming to serve us?" Javix asked after a while.

"It's self-serve," Conrad said, pointing to the sign. "You have to do it yourself."

Javix searched his memory again.

"This body has never done self-serve," he said.

"You want me to do it?" Conrad asked. He'd never pumped gas either, but he was sure he'd figure it out before the alien guy could.

"Yes, you do it," Javix said.

Conrad got out and went to the gas pumps. How hard could it be? Stick the pump into the car and squeeze until the tank was full. Easy. Conrad found the gas cap, and stopped.

"Javix, I need the car keys," he said. "The cap is locked."

Javix tossed him the keys, and Conrad opened the cap and started pumping.

"What's going to happen to my friends?" Conrad asked as he pumped.

"Don't think about them," Javix said.

"I need to know," Conrad said. "They're my friends."

"They're either prisoners," Javix said, "or they're dead."

"Dead?"

"My bet is they're Cyscope's prisoners," Javix said. "He'll contact you when you next fall asleep and tell you to return or he'll kill them. My job is to make sure you don't."

"I want to help them," Conrad said.

"Forget it," Javix said.

Conrad didn't forget it. As he finished filling the tank, he tried to think of what he should do. Javix might have been trying to protect him, but Conrad didn't like him very much. And did Conrad really want to live in a world without Knowlton, his best friend since forever?

No, he didn't. But what could he do? He was just a little kid.

No, he was Hestar, intergalactic adventurer and thief. Would Hestar sit idly by while his friend Gennex was in danger? After all the scrapes Gennex had rescued him from?

No, he would not. Hestar would take action. Hestar would save his friends.

Conrad looked down at the car keys in his hand and smiled.

"Give me your wallet," he said.

"What?" Javix asked.

"I have to pay for the gas," Conrad said. "Give me your wallet."

Javix did some memory searching to find out what a wallet was, then he pulled it out and tossed it to Conrad.

Excellent, Conrad thought. *Now for a distraction.* He walked into the gas station, where an old couple was paying for their gas. Conrad stepped past them and waved up at the manager at the cash register.

"My dad says he's not paying," Conrad said, pointing out the window to where Javix waited in the car. "He says the gas smells funny. And he says you're a crook."

"What?" the manager roared. "I'll fix him!"

The manager stormed out of the station and headed for Javix's car.

Perfect, Conrad thought. *Now, if only I can find a ride back to Toronto.*

"Well, let's get driving," said the old man as he and his wife left the store. "Toronto won't come to us."

Conrad followed them, listening as they walked towards a large camper, the wheels turning in his head.

"Do check the living space in the camper, dear," the old woman said. "One of those filthy hitch-hikers could be hiding in there."

"Now that's just foolishness, woman!" the old man said.

"But the back door doesn't lock properly!" the old woman said. "Anyone could just climb aboard."

"And why would they do that?" the old man said, opening the front door and climbing into the driver's seat.

"They might want to steal all those choco-lates we bought for the grandchildren," his wife said as she climbed in the passenger side.

The camper pulled out of the parking lot and joined the westbound traffic heading for Toronto. Conrad stood by the back door of the camper, watching a heated argument between Javix and the gas station manager, with more than a little amusement.

When the gas station was out of sight, Conrad opened the door a crack and dropped Javix's car keys onto the highway. Satisfied, he turned and looked for a place to sit.

The camper was fairly small, larger than a van but not nearly as spacious as a trailer. A tight corridor led from the front seats to the dining space and the back door, where Conrad stood amongst the luggage. There were also, as promised, several boxes of chocolates.

Conrad sat down between two large suit-cases, opened a box of chocolates, and started eating. He felt a little bad about stealing candy from the people who were giving him a lift. After all, that certainly wasn't what Captain Lassiter would have done. However, if he was to believe his past life, he'd been a thief. Stealing chocolates was simply part of his character.

Or was it? If he felt bad about stealing, then he wasn't a thief any longer. Of course, he wasn't a space adventurer any longer, either, yet here he was engaging himself in a rescue mission. Just like Captain Lassiter in Episode 24. His friends were in the clutches of a body-hopping psycho, and only Hestar could save them.

He was Hestar and he had a job to do, with no time for moral arguments about the ethics of stealing candy. He snatched up another box and continued stuffing his face.

Chapter Thirteen

After he'd eaten his fill of chocolate, Conrad thought about what he would do when he got back to the city. He would go in with his soul-blade blazing, defeat Cyscope and all his cronies, and save all his friends. Perfect plan, except . . .

Except, Conrad had no idea how to begin. He didn't know where they were, and he certainly didn't know how he would defeat all those Hunters. Sure, he had his soulblade, but they all had them, too.

What could he do? What would Captain Lassiter do? For that matter, what had Captain Lassiter done in Episode 24? He had gone in to rescue some trapped colonists from a planet that was about to explode. Cool episode, but not that helpful.

Conrad thought back over the other shows, trying to find a story that matched his situation. There was Episode 12 of *The New Fate*, when Captain Wong was trapped alone on his ship with a handful of ruthless energy thieves. That had also been a good one, but Captain Wong had been able to hide from the thieves. Cyscope could trace Conrad's soul. That was why Javix wanted them to keep moving.

How had Cyscope done that soul tracing, anyway?

Conrad thought about it. Cyscope had found him twice by sensing his soul. Could he, Conrad, do the same?

Conrad closed his eyes and focused. At least, he tried to focus. It seemed to be a situation in which focusing was required, but what was he supposed to focus on?

Cyscope. He should focus on Cyscope. Maybe he'd get an image of him or something, complete with a mailing address and phone number.

Hey, it was worth a shot.

Conrad sat and focused on his enemy, and waited for something to happen.

Cyscope was eating pizza when something happened. His head shot up, his face twitched, and he said:

"Well, well, well."

Cyscope, Quaz, Eelt, Vellen, and John sat around the table in John's house, eating the meal he'd ordered for them. Cyscope had instructed him to prepare something quick and filling, and was finding Hawaiian pizza much to his liking.

"Well what, sir?" Quaz asked.

"The quarry," Cyscope said, "has made contact. Excuse me."

Cyscope put down his slice of Hawaiian, put his hands together, and closed his eyes.

"Hello, Hestar."

"What?" Conrad said, looking this way and that for the source of the voice. He floated in a dark void, devoid of light and substance. However, he could make out the hovering form of an alien head in front of him.

"You!" he said, recognizing the alien head. "Cyscope."

"I am the one you wished to contact," Cyscope said, "am I not?"

"No," Conrad said. "I was just . . . hey! I'm not telling you. You're the bad guy."

Cyscope's disembodied head chuckled at that.

"I have come to this world to find you, Hestar, so that I can find something you stole," he said. "If that makes me the villain, you haven't been taught right from wrong very well."

"I didn't steal any . . . " Conrad began, then stopped. "Well, not in this life," he admitted.

"Call it karma, Hestar," Cyscope said. "You are accountable for all your lives, and all you have done in them."

"Look who's talking," Conrad fired back, poking a finger at Cyscope's reptilian nose. "You torture people. And you killed my friends."

"I have not killed your friends."

"Kidnapped them, then."

"Yes," Cyscope said. "I have one of them here, and the other two will be in my custody very shortly. I was going to contact you, actually."

"Yeah?" Conrad said.

"I offer a trade," Cyscope said.

"Huh," Conrad replied. "That's just what Javix said you'd say."

"Javix?" Cyscope said, interested. "So he's the one who snatched you, is he?"

Oops, Conrad thought. *I shouldn't have told him that.*

"But you did," Cyscope replied.

"Hey!" Conrad said. "I was just thinking that. It wasn't supposed to be out loud."

"All thoughts are aloud here, Hestar," Cyscope told him. "Do you not remember?"

"No."

"It matters not," Cyscope said. "This is what I offer: your friends for the information I want."

"That's it?"

"That's it."

"How do I know I can trust you?" Conrad asked.

"You're the thief, Hestar," Cyscope reminded him. "How do I know I can trust you?"

"Okay, good point," Conrad admitted.

"Shall we trade?"

"Let me think about it," Conrad said. "I'll get back to you."

With a thought, Conrad broke the mental connection. He opened his eyes and found himself back in the camper.

"Wow," he said, then closed his mouth quickly.

"Did you hear that?" said the old lady in the front of the camper.

"Did I hear what?" said the old man driving the camper.

"I heard someone say 'wow' just now," said the old woman.

"It was the wind, that's all," said the old man.

"Oh," said the old woman.

"Whew," said Conrad.

"What was that?" the old woman said.

"The wind," Conrad said quickly.

"Oh," said the old woman. "I'd better roll my window up."

Conrad got to thinking. By focusing on Cyscope he had made contact with him on the spiritual plane. Not what he'd wanted, but he had learned some interesting news.

Cyscope didn't have all his friends yet. Conrad couldn't be sure, but he felt certain Knowlton was still on the loose.

But for how long? Cyscope seemed certain he'd have all Conrad's friends in his hands very soon. All the more reason for me to get back to the city and save them, Conrad thought.

Because this was all his fault. Well, it was Hestar's fault really, but Conrad was Hestar. Cyscope was right—it was karma, or something like it. He was responsible for his past lives.

Hestar had stolen something really important. That must have been why Cyscope had been torturing him in that memory. Hestar had escaped with the help of his friends, but something must have happened. Something that had led to his soul travelling across space and being born on Earth as Conrad.

Conrad needed to find out about that. But who could tell him? Maybe Javix, but he was probably not in the best of moods right now.

Who, then?

"Pakfrida!" Conrad said, snapping his fingers.

"I know I heard something that time," the old lady said.

"No you didn't," Conrad said.

"Perhaps I didn't," she said.

Conrad closed his eyes once more, and focused his mind on the alien named Pakfrida. His world shifted, and he suddenly found himself on the bridge of the Destiny. He sat in the captain's chair, and the face of Pakfrida appeared on the bridge's main viewscreen.

"Hello, Hestar," Pakfrida said. "I was hoping you'd call."

"Call us if you hear anything," said the officer, handing Knowlton's mother his card. "We'll keep you posted from our end."

Knowlton watched as the two police officers turned and left. He and Lysta had given the officers their statements, then listened as they explained the situation. The cops had said there was nothing they could do except wait for the kidnappers to make contact. If they made contact at all.

Knowlton knew there would be no ransom demand. This wasn't about money. This was about something in Conrad's head.

The police might find the aliens, but they would not be prepared for the soulblades. Only he and Lysta knew the real score. Which meant, of course, that if Lysta's mom was to be rescued, it would be up to Lysta and him.

Mostly him, Knowlton thought. After all, he was Gennex, best friend to Hestar the intergalactic hero. If anyone could do it, it was him.

"Knowlton!" snapped his dad, knocking him out of his thoughts. "Pay attention to your mother."

"What?" Knowlton said, looking at his parents.

"I said," his mother said, "go and put fresh sheets on your bed. Lysta will be staying with us tonight, and she will have your room. And make sure you tidy up in there."

"Do like your mother tells you," Knowlton's dad said before his son had a chance to move. "Right now."

"I'm on it," Knowlton said, hurrying to his room.

"Have it ready in half an hour," his mom called after him. "Then you can explain why you chose to miss school."

"I'll help you, Knowlton," Lysta said, rising from the sofa.

"He can do it himself," Knowlton's mother said. "Let me get you some more tea. Burt!"

"Yes, dear," Knowlton's father said, standing quickly and hurrying to the kitchen.

"It will be all right, dear," Knowlton's mother said. She patted Lysta's knee, and Lysta jerked back involuntarily.

"Uh . . . thanks," she said quickly.

"You're welcome, dear," Knowlton's mom said. "Stay as long as you need."

"I need to know what's going on," Conrad said. "No more cryptic dream stuff. Just give it to me straight."

"I would have been happy to tell you everything," Pakfrida said, "on board my ship. You should not have left Javix."

"Well, I did," Conrad said. "And I'm going to rescue my friends. But I need help to do it. I need to know how to find Cyscope the way he keeps finding me."

"A simple technique," Pakfrida said, "which I taught you many years ago. You must try to remember your past life, Hestar."

"That's kinda why I'm talking to you," Conrad said, getting up from the captain's chair and approaching the viewscreen. "You've been trying to contact me for weeks with my dreams, haven't you?"

"Yes, I have," Pakfrida said.

"And I'll bet it was you that possessed my friend Lysta," Conrad went on.

"Correct," Pakfrida said. "The dreams were to prepare you for the truth. I possessed the girl to give you a direct message, something I couldn't do in your dreams without waking you up."

"Huh?" Conrad said, scratching his head. "What do you mean?"

"When I tried to talk to you in your dreams, as we are talking now," Pakfrida explained, "you would wake up. Dreams exist in the subconscious mind, Hestar. Talking to you engages the conscious mind, forcing you out of sleep."

"So that's why I woke up every time things started to get interesting," Conrad said. "Wait a minute, why didn't you just talk to me like this?"

"You weren't ready," Pakfrida told him. "And the contact must be mutual. You didn't know to contact me."

"Oh," said Conrad. "So I can't talk to my friends this way?"

"You could speak to them," Pakfrida said, "but it would only be a voice in the back of their minds."

"Hey!" Conrad said. "When I first ran into Cyscope, I heard a voice telling me to run. Was that you?"

"Yes," Pakfrida said. "I was very concerned for you. I still am, to tell you the truth. You are in great danger."

"Yeah, yeah," Conrad said. "Just tell me how to locate people so I can save my friends."

"Look within yourself, Hestar," Pakfrida said. "Remember your past. If you look, you will find it."

"What?" Conrad said. "I don't understand."

Pakfrida didn't answer. His image vanished from the viewscreen, then the bridge set disappeared.

"Hey!" Conrad said. "Come back."

It was no use. He was back in the camper once more.

"What was that noise?" the old woman asked.

"Still the wind," Conrad replied.

Chapter Fourteen

"You see?" Knowlton's mother said. "Just as good as your bed upstairs."

Knowlton looked at the sleeping bag, spread over the three sofa cushions on the basement floor, and sighed inwardly.

"It looks great, Mom," he said without enthusiasm.

"Don't take that tone of voice with me, young man," his mom said. "I took the trouble to make this bed for you. What do you say?"

"Thank you, Mom."

"That's much better."

Knowlton's mother turned and saw her son's downturned face, and her own features softened slightly.

"I'm sure your friend Connor will turn up safely," she said.

"His name is Conrad," Knowlton said quietly.

"Yes, yes, dear," his mother said. "Now, you get a good night's sleep, and tomorrow we'll make sure you get on that schoolbus."

Yeah, right, Knowlton thought as he sat on his makeshift bed. His parents barely knew he existed in the morning, they were so busy getting ready for their day. If he heard from them at all, it was "Out of the way, dear," or "Hurry up in the bathroom."

"I need some things from my room," Knowlton said, standing back up. "I'll just—"

"You be sure you knock first," his mother said, climbing the stairs back up to the kitchen.

"Your friend Lysta might be changing, and she's had enough fright for one day."

So have I, Knowlton thought as he followed his mother. At least now he knew why she and his dad were so insensitive toward him. He had an alien soul, and Earth people didn't like that.

But they're my parents, he thought. *Shouldn't that count for something?*

When he reached the kitchen he heard the doorbell ring. Not wanting to be chewed out for not answering it, he walked to the front door and opened it.

Zepher and Vorla stood on the doorstep, their soulblades lit and ready.

"Whoa!" Knowlton screamed, slamming the door in their faces. "Mom! Dad! Lysta! We gotta go. Now!"

"Knowlton, what is it?" his mom asked, rushing in from the kitchen.

"The kidnappers!" Knowlton said. "They're here."

As he said the words, the soulblades burst through the door and sliced it apart.

"What's all this noise?" Knowlton's father asked, rushing down the stairs. He stopped when he saw the two girls in the doorway. His mouth flapped as he tried to make sense of it all, but no words came out.

"You will all come with us," Zepher said. "Resist us, and you will die."

Conrad thought he'd died. Then he realized he'd succeeded in making contact with his past. He'd focused, as Pakfrida had suggested, on remembering who he'd been. He'd expected it to lead to nothing, but decided he'd give it a go. What was the harm in trying?

After a few minutes of focusing, Conrad got bored. It hadn't worked, so he stopped and ate more chocolate. He'd nearly finished another box when he'd had a brainstorm.

What had Javix said about reading his possessed body's memories? He'd talked about it being like downloading and reading files.

Could that work? Well, why not? Conrad pretended his mind was a computer, then he clicked on a file marked Hestar. And then . . .

Bam!

Conrad's mind was flooded with images, too many for him to cope with. His mind winked out.

And he had come to an hour later with one brute of a headache and a mind full of new memories. It was weird but it was real—he had memories in his head from a life lived in space!

He looked at a few, taking them in slowly this time. He started with the ones he'd already seen in his dreams. This time, when he saw them, he remembered why he'd been there and what he'd been doing.

The asteroid field. He and his friends Gennex and Tink had just stolen some data disks from one of the Deltran Empire's outer-rim worlds. They'd been chased, and Hestar had taken off on his spacebike to lure them away from the Magnus.

Wow, Conrad thought. *There's a galactic empire out there. And they have outer-rim worlds!*

There was also a resistance organization, known as the Light Movement. *Cool,* Conrad thought. *Just like the Senti movement in the Varo Empire from The New Fate.*

Hestar had been part of that resistance. He'd convinced Gennex to join. He'd met Pakfrida, learned the power he had in his soul. And then . . .

There was something there, something powerful, but he couldn't see what it was. When he tried, feelings of anxiety welled up within him, making him stop. What was that all about?

Conrad decided he would worry about that later. He had his memories back. Now it was time to use those memories to rescue his friends. He had to remember how to track a soul.

He was Hestar, sitting in a small circle of five aliens with an eight-legged, spider-like alien named Bizur squatting in the middle. It was a lesson; Bizur was on Pakfrida's staff of teachers. The room itself was empty and white, and was one of many such rooms in the school. Bright sunlight poured in from windows high up near the ceiling, giving the room an ethereal glow.

"First, you must choose a partner and scan their soul," Bizur said. "Can anyone here tell me how to do a soul scan?"

"By staring at their eyes?" said a student whose skin looked like fish scales.

"Correct! Very good, Lyoza," Bizur said, bouncing a bit on his legs. Conrad knew right then that the spider-like alien bounced and hopped when he was pleased with his students. "Now, it needn't be a deep stare, like you practiced the other day in Gimlor's soul-reading class. This is just to get an image of the soul you will be searching for.

"Go on, then. Find partners."

The students broke into pairs, Hestar pairing himself with a rock-skinned alien named Lolar. At Bizur's instruction, half the class left the classroom to hide somewhere in the building. When five standard minutes had elapsed, Bizur resumed the class.

"Picture your partner in your mind," he said, "then focus on finding them. Don't focus on the person themselves. You only need to do that if you want to contact them. I think Rizta knows what I'm talking about."

"What?" said a squid-like alien, wriggling her tentacles. "Oh, sorry teacher. We were just—"

"Having a little talk, yes," Bizur said. "I'm glad to know you've developed your telepathy, Rizta, but don't forget to pay attention in class.

"Where was I? Ah, yes. Focus on knowing where your partner is. Then trust whatever impulse comes to you. Picture this building in your mind, if that will help."

Hestar focused, trusting his feelings and imagining a cross-section of the building. In seconds, he knew exactly where the rocky alien was.

"Lolar's in the kitchen," he said suddenly, "sitting on a stool near the washbasins."

"Very good, Hestar," Bizur said, hopping once in satisfaction. "That is exactly where your partner is. Well done. Go and fetch him, and then it will be his turn to find you."

"How are the rest of you doing?" he asked the class as Hestar got up to leave.

That's all I need to know, Conrad thought, pulling his mind out of the memory.

He focused on finding Cyscope, picturing the city of Toronto in his mind. It seemed a daunting task to imagine a whole city, but he'd been up the CN Tower a few times and had a good idea of what he needed to see.

Conrad expected the image of the city would glow on the spot where Cyscope was, but it did not. Instead he had a very clear idea in the back of his mind where his enemy was. He didn't know the address or the nearest intersection; Conrad simply knew exactly how far away he was from Cyscope's location.

"Downtown," Conrad said aloud.

"No, we're goin' to Mount Pleasant Road," the old man said.

"I didn't say anything," the old woman replied.

"Must've been the wind again," the old man said. "Better fix those windows when we get there."

Conrad ignored the old couple and did another search. He'd looked into Knowlton's eyes several times, and definitely Lysta's once or twice. He hoped that was enough. Conrad expected to find one of them in the same location as Cyscope, but decided to look anyway. He focused on finding Knowlton first, and instantly he knew.

"Good," Conrad said. "He's at home."

"Of course our son is at home," the old woman said. "He's waiting for us."

So, Conrad thought, *Cyscope doesn't have him yet. Did he have Lysta?* Conrad focused on finding her, and was delighted to find her in the same spot. They were both safe—Cyscope didn't have either of them. But what had he said? 'I'll have them soon enough,' or something to that effect. Maybe the Hunters were out looking for them.

If that was the case, Conrad knew he had to get there first. He looked out the camper's back window, and was delighted to see they were pulling off the Don Valley Parkway onto Eglinton Avenue. In ten minutes they would be on Mount Pleasant Road, only a couple of blocks from his home. He could jump off at the traffic lights, then run to Knowlton's place and check in.

Conrad waited anxiously by the back door, hoping he'd get there in time.

Chapter Fifteen

"What is the meaning of this?" Knowlton's mother demanded of the two teenage girls who had just cut through her front door with soulblades.

"Mom," Knowlton said, raising his voice, "we should really do what these aliens want." It was his hope that Lysta would hear him, and either escape through a window or stay hidden.

"We are here to kidnap you," Vorla said.

"I should think not!" Knowlton's mother said, picking up the telephone handset from a small table. "Burt, throw these two young ladies out of the house. I'm calling the police."

Knowlton's father stepped forward. Zepher flashed her soulblade under his chin, and he stopped. Vorla sliced through the telephone, cutting the cable and chopping the table in half.

Knowlton's mother stared at the energy sword, stunned. Knowlton's father fainted.

Oh, wonderful, Knowlton thought.

"I'm the one you want," he said, stepping toward them and raising his hands. "Leave them alone and I'll come quietly."

"Where is the girl?" Zepher asked him.

"She's not here," Knowlton said, keeping his voice loud. If Lysta had any sense she'd stay out of sight until he'd left with these two aliens.

And if his mom had any sense, she would go along with him and keep quiet.

"Knowlton, you know that's not true!" she said. "The young lady is talking about Lysta."

"Who left ten minutes ago," Knowlton said quickly. "If you hurry, you might just catch her."

"Knowlton, dear!" his mother said. In spite of everything that was going on, she was still managing to be a grown up.

"She left ten minutes ago," Knowlton repeated, glaring at his mother and winking furiously. "She went with the police to answer some more questions. Didn't she, Mother?"

"No she didn't!" his mother said.

"Yes she did," Knowlton said, nodding for extra emphasis.

"I'll search the house," Vorla said, and she turned and bounded up the stairs. Zepher kept her soulblade trained on Knowlton.

Not good, Knowlton thought, listening to a commotion coming from upstairs. Had Lysta found a way to escape? It sounded like she was in his parents' bedroom.

There were footsteps on the roof, then Lysta dropped down into view in front of the living room window. She ran off into the night, and a moment later the alien girl dropped down from the roof and chased after her.

"Awright, Lysta!" Knowlton said, punching the air.

"She won't get far, boy," Zepher said.

Lysta ran like her life depended on it. Which, she thought, it probably did. The street ended at the entrance to a park, and she ran into it and looked around for somewhere to hide.

There was a children's play structure directly ahead, with plastic slides and wooden plank floors and walls. Beyond the play structure she saw a ravine behind a wire-mesh fence. The ravine would be a great hiding place, but it would take too much time to climb the fence. Her pursuer didn't need to climb, not when she could cut through the fence with that sword of hers.

On the other hand, the play structure was way too obvious. Still, it was the best option. Lysta had a slight lead on the alien girl, and would have just enough time to hide in the structure before she entered the park.

Lysta dove under the play structure and pulled herself along through the sand. She hid herself behind a wooden slat, then looked at

the orange tube slide to her left. It would give
her better cover, but she would not be able to
see the alien coming.

And, she was out of time. Vorla sprinted
into the park and stopped, then looked all
around. Lysta breathed in relief; the alien
didn't know where she was.

Yet.

Conrad waited until the camper stopped at the
traffic lights, then he jumped up and leapt out
the door. He ignored the surprised cries from
the old couple and ran off as fast as he could.

He did a quick check on his friends' loca-
tions. Knowlton was still at his house, but
Lysta was a lot closer. Probably in the park just
up ahead.

Conrad ran faster, and was almost to the
park when he realized he wasn't limping. The
second he made that realization, the pain in
his leg returned. Big time.

"Ow!" Conrad cried, stumbling and falling
face-first. He picked himself up and hobbled
off, and tried very hard to run again.

Come on, he scolded himself. Hestar wouldn't let a little thing like a hurt leg stop him! Hestar would ignore the pain and do what had to be done.

"I'm not Hestar anymore," Conrad said aloud, and wondered where that thought had come from. Of course he was Hestar! He had to be. After all, Conrad was just a weak little kid that nobody liked.

"That's not true!" Conrad said, then shook his head. Now was not the time for an identity crisis!

Conrad entered the park. Ignoring the pain as best he could, he forced his legs to start running.

The Hunter crouched and scanned the ground. A moment or so later she started walking, heading straight for the wooden play structure.

Lysta willed herself to remain quiet and still. She wanted to move, to rush to a better spot, but she knew she'd be seen. Her heart pounded, her breath locked itself in her chest, as Vorla closed in.

The Hunter crouched again, studying the sand around the structure. Lysta realized too late that her footprints were clearly visible. She might as well have drawn an arrow in the sand, pointing to her location. The Hunter's head snapped up suddenly, locked eyes with Lysta, and she smiled.

"Got you," Vorla said. "Come on out, or I'll cut you out."

"Cut this!"

Lysta looked up as footfalls hammered past above her, and then the teenage Hunter was fighting with someone. Lysta squirmed out from under the structure and got a better look, and couldn't believe her eyes.

It was Conrad. He was back, dueling with the alien with his light sword. As she watched them fight, Lysta was no longer afraid. Conrad fought with a skill and fury she hadn't known he possessed. The tables were turned, and the Hunter was now the hunted.

Conrad drove Vorla back, feeling his power fueling him as he fought. The alien was on the defensive; she managed to block Conrad's blows, but had no opening to launch an attack of her own. She backed off, hoping to buy herself a second, but her opponent refused to give it to her.

Conrad wasn't surprised at all by his skill now—he'd looked into his memories and relived all his training days with the alien Pakfrida. He'd been the top fighter in his class, rivaling even his teacher.

The alien-possessed girl had no chance. She retreated until her back was touching the fence blocking the ravine. Vorla cut her way through and tried to run, but her foot caught in a root and she tumbled down into the ravine.

Conrad was right behind her. He leapt after the tumbling teen, soulblade blazing, ready to finish her off. A dozen memories from his past life flashed in his mind, scenes where Hestar had fought and defeated several of the Deltran Empire's greatest assassins. This would be just like those times.

Except, Conrad realized, it wouldn't be. He'd been Hestar then, and even though Hestar was okay with that kind of stuff, he was Conrad now. As he stood over Vorla, the point of his soulblade under her chin, memories of a different sort filled his mind. He remembered several episodes of *Infinite Destiny*, both old and new, where he'd learned that killing was wrong.

Conrad lowered his soulblade. He wasn't a murderer.

"Get up," he instructed, and the alien got up.

Then she lashed out with her hand, slapping him across his left cheek. Conrad stumbled back, then caught his bad leg in a hole and fell forwards.

"Ullk . . ." Vorla said.

Conrad backed away, his soulblade vanishing. His leg hurt, but he barely noticed it. All he saw was the wound in the middle of the girl's chest.

Vorla looked down at her wound, then up at Conrad. Their eyes met, and Conrad was blasted into another of Hestar's memories.

It was the corridor dream again, just after he'd been tortured by Cyscope, then rescued by Gennex and Tink. Hestar charged down the corridor, blasting at any alien that came his way, feeling indestructible. Conrad loved this dream, loved the feeling of power he got. It was like he was in an arcade game, playing a first-person shooter, and he was winning.

There was a movement to Hestar's right and suddenly he was in agony. He collapsed to the floor and looked at his legs, and saw his right one was missing below the knee. Above him stood a being with a soulblade, a being Conrad knew to be the teen girl Hunter, Vorla.

Conrad flashed back to the present, where he was still staring into the girl's eyes.

"I suppose . . . we are even . . . Hestar," Vorla said, then she fell backwards into the stream at the bottom of the ravine.

Chapter Sixteen

"He has returned to the city," said Quaz. "Why? He could have evaded us if . . ."

"Silence," Cyscope said. He sat in an armchair, his hands folded across his chest, his eyes closed.

Cyscope had sensed Vorla's death. It mattered little to him. She would find a new body soon enough. What was significant, however, was that Conrad had crossed a line. A line that, once crossed, could not be stepped back over.

Hestar had killed many victims, as Cyscope well knew, having been one of them. But Conrad? No. It was entirely likely the boy would be scarred for life, assuming he had much of a life left to him.

Not if I catch him, Cyscope thought.

"He has returned to rescue his friends," Cyscope said, opening his eyes. "They are his weakness and we shall exploit it."

"Hmm," Quaz said, looking over at the chairs where Lysta's mom and John's wife were tied. "I say we kill them now and be done with it."

Cyscope turned and idly viewed their captives. John's wife was a nuisance, but John had begged him to spare her. She might be useful for controlling John, if the need arose. Lysta's mother had no real value now that they had Gennex. However . . .

"We do not know how many of Hestar's abilities have resurfaced," Cyscope said. "He might detect their deaths, and then our advantage would be lost."

"Kill one of them," Quaz said. "Show him we mean business."

Cyscope looked at his junior officer. He smiled at him. Then he sprang to his feet and slugged Quaz hard in the stomach.

"When I want your opinion, Quaz," Cyscope said, "I'll ask for it. Otherwise, keep your mouth shut. Am I clear on this?"

"Yes, sir," Quaz gasped, doubled over on the floor.

"We have the girl's mother, and we have Gennex," Cyscope said. "Hestar will come to us. Of this I am certain."

"What of the rogue agent, Javix?" Vellen asked. "He may return."

"If he does," Cyscope said, "he will be dealt with."

Slowly, zombie-like, Conrad climbed up out of the ravine. Lysta ran to him, asked him what had happened.

Conrad pointed over his shoulder and kept walking. Lysta looked down into the ravine, saw the body, and gasped.

"Conrad?" she said, running to catch up with him. "Conrad, did you—"

"It was an accident, I swear," Conrad said. "I tripped, fell forward and . . ." Conrad stopped, suddenly unable to talk.

"Conrad, it's okay," Lysta said, putting a hand on his shoulder. "You fought her to save me. You did what you had to."

"I killed her," Conrad said. "That's two people I've killed today!"

"You mean that guy in the pajamas?" Lysta asked. "That was an accident as well. I saw it in your mind, remember? Besides, they were after you. Neither of them would have died if they hadn't forced you to defend yourself."

"I guess," Conrad said. "Of course, they're not really dead."

"What do you mean?" Lysta asked.

Conrad explained what he knew of possession as they walked back to Knowlton's house. It was slow going; after that flashback, his leg hurt worse than ever. Conrad also told her some of what he'd learned from Javix, Pak-frida, and his own memory searching.

"That's why this is happening," Conrad said as they approached the destroyed front door. "Cyscope's after something I stole, and Pakfrida's trying to make sure he doesn't get it."

"What was it you stole?" Lysta asked.

"I haven't remembered that part yet," Conrad said.

They went inside and looked around, calling Knowlton's name and hoping against common sense that someone would still be there. It was useless. Knowlton and his parents were long gone.

"Cyscope has them now," Conrad said, flopping down in a living room chair. "Knowlton, his parents, your mom—"

"At least he doesn't have your mom yet," Lysta said.

Conrad looked up at her, his face a mask of horror.

"Oh, no," Lysta said.

Conrad was already hobbling for the door.

"Mom?" Conrad shouted as he rushed into his house. "Mom, where are you?"

The computer was still on, with a half-finished game of solitaire on the screen. There was an empty beer bottle on the table beside the computer, and the chair had fallen over backwards.

Conrad hobbled over to the computer. The timer in the bottom of the solitaire game said four minutes, twenty-seven seconds. One of the many cigarette butts in the ashtray was still smoking.

"Mom?" Conrad called, turning around.

His mother stood by the door, clutching Lysta to her chest with one hand and holding a soulblade under her chin with the other.

"Mom?" Conrad said, but he knew the woman was no longer his mother. It was her body, but it had been possessed. His mother's spirit was gone.

"Oh, Mom," Conrad said.

"What a lucky coincidence," said Vorla through Conrad's mother's mouth. "The nearest body ripe for possession happened to be your mother. She barely struggled at all when I took her over. In fact, she welcomed the release."

"Shut up," Conrad said.

"She must have been desperate to get away from you," Vorla sneered.

"Shut up!" Conrad shouted, his soulblade crackling to life in his hand.

"Put that down, boy," the Hunter warned, burning a small spot on Lysta's chin.

"Ow!" Lysta cried, straining her neck to keep out of the soulblade's reach.

Conrad opened his fist and his blade disappeared.

"You will come with me now," Vorla said. "If you resist, I will kill the girl."

Conrad took a moment to absorb the situation. His mother, whom he'd known all his life, was gone. They hadn't been very close, but she had been his mother on this world and he had loved her. She'd kept him fed, given him a roof over his head, and the means to tape his favorite show. She hadn't been great, but she'd been there.

But not any more. Life, as Conrad had known it, would never be the same.

All he had left were his friends, and he was in danger of losing them, too. He tried to think of what Hestar would do, then decided that didn't really matter. He had one choice if he wanted to rescue his friends—he would have to play along, and surrender himself to Vorla.

"Take me to Cyscope," Conrad said, "and I'll tell him what he wants to know."

Chapter Seventeen

Knowlton tugged uselessly at the ropes binding him to the chair. He knew he couldn't get himself free, but the noises he made were clearly irritating Quaz, their lone guard. Knowlton's parents were tied to the chairs beside him, as were Lysta's mom and John's wife.

Knowlton's parents were the only ones who were gagged. The alien leader—Cyscope—had taped their mouths shut after only five minutes of them being brought in. It seemed Cyscope couldn't stand their constant verbal abuse any more than Knowlton could.

Knowlton had almost thanked him. Almost. His parents were still his parents, after all. They'd raised him, taught him right from wrong. Of course, wrong was whatever it was he was doing, and right was anything they did. But they had made an effort, and they let him watch *Infinite Destiny*, so they weren't all bad.

Besides, Cyscope was a crazy alien scumbag who wanted some secret that Conrad had in his head. Knowlton redoubled his efforts at struggling, trying to be as noisy as possible.

"Stop that," said Quaz. The burns he'd received in the fire at Lysta's place looked very painful, and added to Knowlton's amusement.

"I am merely trying to get comfortable," Knowlton said innocently.

"You're not supposed to be comfortable," Quaz said, glaring at him. "You're supposed to be quiet."

"I'm so very sorry to have disturbed you," Knowlton said. "I will sit still in this position from now on."

Quaz grunted and looked away. Knowlton squeezed his ropes rhythmically, in time with his breathing. Before long the squeaking this caused got on Quaz's nerves again.

"I said no noise," Quaz said, standing up and glowering at Knowlton.

"I'm sorry," Knowlton said, "but you insisted I sit in this position and not move. Unfortunately my breathing is putting pressure on the ropes. I could shift around to stop it, but you insisted—"

"All right, all right, move to a different position," Quaz said. "Just be quiet about it. Or I'll solve the problem myself by stopping your breathing."

"Okay, okay! Calm down," Knowlton said, shifting around quietly in his chair. He looked at the others and had to suppress a giggle. They were looking at him in horror, as if they couldn't believe the trouble he was inviting on himself. His parents looked completely mortified. If they weren't gagged, Knowlton thought, they'd probably tell him to sit still and be polite to the alien-possessed kidnapper.

Knowlton made himself comfortable, settling into position with a loud skreeeeeeeccchhh.

"That does it!" Quaz roared, storming towards Knowlton with his soulblade lit.

Whoops, Knowlton thought. *Maybe I went a bit too far that time.*

"Quaz," Cyscope called from the doorway, just as the alien was about to strike. "I want the hostages undamaged."

"Yes, sir," Quaz grunted, his soulblade dissipating.

"Bring that one in here," Cyscope said, returning to the kitchen. "I will speak with him."

"As you wish," Quaz said, hefting Knowlton, chair and all, off the floor. "When this is over," he whispered in Knowlton's ear as he carried him, "I will kill you very, very slowly."

"Yeah, yeah," Knowlton said. "I get that a lot."

Quaz slammed Knowlton's chair down at the kitchen table, sneered at him, then stomped out.

"Enjoying yourself, Gennex?" Cyscope said, peeling an orange. He'd become quite fond of oranges.

"Who?" Knowlton said. "Oh, right. The alien guy. People around here call me The Know."

"Do they?" Cyscope flicked a bit of orange peel across the table. "And what do you know about your past life, Know?"

"Not a thing," Knowlton said. "When I found out I was this Gennex guy, I was as surprised as anything. It's Conrad who's been having the cool dreams."

"Messages," Cyscope said. "He is wanted by many different parties besides myself. I imagine someone was trying to jog his memory."

"Yeah, because he knows about something that every alien worth his probe would give both his bug eyes for," Knowlton said. "What is it, anyway?"

"Hestar hasn't told you?" Cyscope asked, chewing his orange.

"I don't think even he knows," Knowlton said.

"Oh, he does," Cyscope said. "The question is, do you?"

"I just said—"

"You were Hestar's closest friend," Cyscope said. "If he would have told anyone his secret, it would have been you."

"If you say so."

Cyscope slammed his hand down on the table, making Knowlton jump.

"Show some respect, boy," the alien snapped. "Your life is in my hands, and when I have Hestar I will not need you, or your parents, any longer. What I do with you at that point depends entirely on how helpful you are to me now. Do I make myself clear?"

"Yes," Knowlton said quickly. "Very clear."

"Good," Cyscope said. "I am going to scan your soul's memories. Hide nothing from me, and when I have your friend you will be free to go. Resist me in any way and you will watch your parents die. Do you understand?"

"I understand," Knowlton said. "Can I use the bathroom first?"

"No," Cyscope said. He reached across the table to take Knowlton's face in his hands, and stopped.

"One moment," he said, and closed his eyes and put his hands together as if in prayer. Knowlton watched him, puzzled, for half a minute. Then, as suddenly as his trance had begun, it ended.

"Good news," Cyscope said. "Hestar has been captured. One of my Hunters is bringing him in."

"Oh good," Knowlton said without enthusiasm.

"Now," Cyscope said, taking Knowlton's head in his hands, "where were we?"

Cyscope stared into Knowlton's eyes, and saw the secrets of his soul.

Conrad and Lysta sat in the back of Conrad's mother's car while Vorla drove them across town. They sat in silence. Conrad stared into his lap, defeated. Lysta stared out the window, feeling awful. If she'd only been careful, maybe that Hunter wouldn't have caught her. She turned to look at Conrad, and couldn't help but catch the top thoughts in his head.

Oh man, Lysta thought. *And I thought I felt bad.*

Conrad's thoughts were a mess of self-pity and self blame. He felt very badly about the loss of his mother, but his primary thoughts were more confusing. He blamed himself for their current predicament, and was sure things would have turned out differently if he'd only been Hestar. That didn't make sense to Lysta. Conrad was Hestar, wasn't he?

"You did everything you could have done," she said, patting Conrad's shoulder.

"Hestar wouldn't have surrendered," he replied, not looking at her. "He would have found a way to win."

"We're not down yet," Lysta said. "We'll get out of this somehow."

"No, you won't," Vorla said, eyeing them in the rearview mirror. "Quiet now. We're almost there."

It hadn't been a long trip—Cyscope's home base was halfway between Conrad's home and his school. Ironically, it was about half a block from where Cyscope's previous body had been killed.

As they turned that very corner, another car rammed them and knocked them off the road. Their car slammed into what was left of the lamppost Conrad had cut in half that morning, and stopped with a sickening jolt.

"Ungh," Conrad said, fingering the seatbelt that had saved his life. Lysta, also wearing her belt, was likewise shaken but unhurt.

The Hunter was a different story. Vorla hadn't been wearing a belt, and was leaning very still across the steering wheel.

"Oh, no," Conrad said, unbuckling himself and climbing into the front seat. There was blood on the steering wheel, and both of Vorla's arms looked broken.

Before Conrad could check to see if she was alive, the driver's side door opened and hands grabbed her and pulled her out of the car.

"Hey!" Conrad shouted, climbing after her. A man stood over Vorla, checking her neck for a pulse.

Suddenly the man turned and grabbed Conrad by both arms. As he did so, Conrad recognized him.

"Javix!" Conrad said.

"You're pretty slippery, kid," the alien bounty hunter said, "but I've got you this time."

Chapter Eighteen

Cyscope removed his hands from Knowlton's head. His soul and memory search had lasted less than five seconds, and what it had revealed astonished him.

"It can't be," Cyscope said.

Knowlton sat stunned, his mind a fog of past life memories, his brain trying desperately to sort them.

Cyscope stared at Knowlton and a smile spread across his features.

"Well, well," he said.

Before he could say more, Zepher ran into the room.

"Admiral Cyscope, we have trouble," she said. "Javix is back, and he has the quarry."

"Quaz, guard the prisoners," Cyscope commanded, his soul already locked on to Conrad's position. "The rest of you with me. It is time we ended this."

Cyscope, the soldier, John, and the remaining Hunters ran for the front door and left in a hurry. Knowlton watched them go, his mind starting to sort itself out. He had one clear thought:

With Cyscope gone, there was no one to protect him from Quaz.

"Alone at last," the alien said, poking his burned face around the corner into the kitchen. "Cyscope was hoping you might have some information in your head, wasn't he? Can I assume he didn't get it?"

"If you want," Knowlton said, struggling to keep his face neutral. He remembered the Hunter's promise about killing him slowly.

"Isn't that a shame," Quaz said, and he grabbed Knowlton's chair and picked him up. "If he got nothing from you, then you are of no further use to us."

Quaz carried Knowlton back into the living room. When he arrived, he raised Knowlton up even higher, then threw him hard into the floor. Lysta's mother and John's wife screamed. Knowlton's parents made muffled noises behind their gags. Knowlton moaned in pain.

"You are at my mercy," Quaz pointed out. "Just the way I want it."

"I don't care what you want," Javix said, dragging Conrad toward his car. "You are coming with me, now!"

"Let go, you jerk!" Conrad said, struggling to free his hands from Javix's grip. "I'm not going with you."

"Leave him alone," Lysta said, running around the car and grabbing Javix's arm.

"What are you complaining about?" Javix said, looking down at her. "I just rescued you from a Hunter. For free!"

"He's a bounty hunter," Conrad explained, seeing the confusion in Lysta's face. "He was hired to rescue me and get me to a space ship."

"Oh," Lysta said. "Oh! You were the one who saved Conrad this afternoon outside my place."

"Correct," Javix said. "Now, if we've finished chatting—"

"Not yet," Conrad said, stomping his bad leg down on one of Javix's feet. It hurt him to do it, but Conrad ignored the pain.

Javix did not. He howled and let go of Conrad, who promptly stomped on the other one.

"Ow!" Javix roared, hopping mad. "You little . . ." he began, and stopped. Conrad's soulblade was right under his chin.

"You listen to me," Conrad said. "I don't care who you are or who paid you, or even what's going on with my past life. I am going to go and save my friend, his parents, and

Lysta's mom. I could use your help, but if you're only going to get in my way," he tried to remember what Vognon, the tactical officer from the Destiny, would have said, "then I will strike you down. Do you understand?"

Javix stared at Conrad, fury coating his face like a wet cloth. Conrad stared right back at him, the soulblade steady under Javix's chin. Lysta watched them both, waiting for something to happen.

"I don't mean to interrupt," she said after a few moments of tense staring, "but could we sort this out now? We might not have much time left."

"You are absolutely right, girl."

Conrad, Javix, and Lysta spun around. Cyscope stood behind them, and his Hunters had them surrounded.

"This ends now," Cyscope said. "Bring the boy to me. Kill the rest."

"Here we go again," Conrad said, turning to Javix. "Go on, light up your soulblade."

"I can't," Javix replied.

"What do you mean, you can't?" Conrad asked, watching as the Hunters closed in.

"I mean I can't, kid," he said. "I don't have that skill."

"Oh, great," Conrad said.

And then the Hunters were upon them.

"They're upon them now," Quaz said, looking out the window at the battle at the end of the block. "I imagine Javix and the little girl," he cast a mocking look at Lysta's mother, "will be dead by the end of this minute."

"Leave her alone," Knowlton groaned from the floor. He still lay where Quaz had thrown him, tears running down his face.

"You are in no position to make demands, boy," Quaz said, walking over to him. "Just the opposite, in fact. Soon he will have Hestar, and when that happens, Cyscope will order your deaths."

Quaz bent low over Knowlton, smiling at him. "So it makes no difference if I kill you now," he said.

"I suppose not," Knowlton said, staring up into Quaz's eyes. His mind hadn't been the same since he'd had that brain-drain from

Cyscope. He'd seen visions of another life, images he hadn't understood at all. He felt sure he would have made sense of them if only he'd had a few more minutes to himself. It did not look like he was going to get them, though.

However, he was not going to let this flame-broiled alien kill him, either. When Quaz had thrown him to the floor, the chair had snapped in several places. Knowlton had used the last several minutes to try and work his hands free from the ropes, and he finally managed to get his left wrist out.

Knowlton grabbed the back of his chair and swung it like a club. It connected solidly with the side of Quaz's head, and he staggered back, stunned.

Knowlton scrambled to his feet. His legs were still tied to the legs of the chair, two of which were still attached to the seat. It was awkward for him to move, and put him at a serious disadvantage. If Quaz attacked now, Knowlton knew he would not be able to defend himself.

He didn't have to. As Quaz staggered back, Lysta's mother jumped her chair forward and tripped him up. Quaz landed on the floor between Lysta's mom and Knowlton's mother. Knowlton's dad threw himself sideways with all his strength, hitting his wife's chair with almost enough force to knock it over. Knowlton's mother did not look pleased at all, especially not when Knowlton hopped over and helped his father tip her chair the rest of the way. She landed on top of Quaz, squashing the breath out of him and pinning him to the floor.

"Good job, Dad!" Knowlton said, pulling off his father's gag.

"He deserved it," his father replied. "Knowlton, what is going on here?"

"I don't have time to explain," Knowlton said, freeing himself from his ropes and then working to free his father. "Let's just say Conrad and I are . . . special. And these guys want us because of that specialness."

"I still don't understand," his father said, standing up and rubbing his wrists.

"You don't have to," Knowlton said. "Well, gotta go. Got a universe to save."

Knowlton ran to the door, then turned around.

"Goodbye, Dad. Bye, Mom," he said, staring at them for a moment or two.

"Goodbye, son," his father said as Knowlton ran through the doorway into the night.

Chapter Nineteen

Conrad threw himself into the fray, soulblade slicing the air and forcing the Hunters to back off. Javix backed him up, springing forward and catching one of the old men by surprise. *Good*, Conrad thought, watching Javix land a solid punch under Eelt's chin. He'd been afraid he would have to carry the entire fight himself.

Zepher challenged Conrad, meeting his soulblade with her own. She slashed, forcing him back into his mom's car, then drove her soulblade forward in a stab. Conrad dodged, leaning back onto the car's hood, then kicked both feet into Zepher's chest. The teen girl staggered back, and Conrad mentally congratulated himself on a cool move as he went after her.

"Come and get it," Conrad cried, letting Hestar's instincts take over.

Vellen, the second old man, moved in. Conrad spun away from Zepher and somersaulted between the two cars, cutting the old man's belt as he went. Vellen's pants fell down, and Conrad suppressed a giggle as he watched him struggle to pull them back up.

Zepher tried to get past the old man but could not; Javix's car was on one side, Conrad's mom's car on the other, with Vellen in the way. Conrad had a second to catch his breath and assess the situation.

Eelt was down. Javix struggled with a man Conrad hadn't seen before, one who didn't have a soulblade. Lysta crouched behind Javix's car, staying out of the way. Vorla, the Hunter in

Conrad's mom's body, lay still on the pavement behind him.

And Cyscope merely stood by, watching the fight.

The second was up. Zepher cut through Vellen's pants, then they turned and advanced on Conrad. They swung their blades and Conrad blocked, then he fought back hard. It was quite a thing, taking on two people at once. Both were skilled fighters, and gave Conrad all they had.

While blocking a lunge from Zepher, Vellen made it past Conrad's defense and slashed his left shoulder. Conrad cried out and backed off, clutching his scorched wound.

"Careful, fool!" Cyscope shouted. "I want him alive, remember. Stunning force only."

Stunning force, Conrad thought. *What did that mean?* He looked at the advancing Hunters and saw their soulblades change color slightly. It prompted a memory from his past life, where Pakfrida had taught him to create and control his soulblade.

"Remember, your soulblade extends from your soul," his mentor had said. "It is a part of you, and as such it responds to your wishes. You can change the intensity of the beam to suit your needs of the moment."

Pakfrida had taught the class how to manipulate their soulblades for all purposes. At the highest intensity, a blade could kill with a mere touch. At medium intensity, it could cut through all but the strongest substances. At a lower intensity, it could stun.

Conrad reviewed the memory of that class in an instant, then he lowered his blade's intensity until it was the same color as his attackers'. Relief flooded through him; he didn't have to kill! He only wished he'd had that memory sooner. If he had, he could have stunned Vorla when she'd been in the teen girl's body, and his mother might still be alive.

Instead of on the ground behind him.

Now wasn't the time to think of such things. Conrad leapt back into the fight, forcing the two Hunters to retreat. He remembered every battle he'd ever been in, every time he'd had to raise his soulblade to an enemy, and he brought every move he knew into play.

In moments he made it past Vellen's defense and slashed him up the chest. The man's body remained undamaged, but he collapsed to the pavement out cold.

Zepher braced herself for Conrad's next attack, then she collapsed as well. Behind her stood Lysta, holding a baseball bat.

"Good job!" Conrad said.

"Handy," Lysta said, "how there's always one of these around when you need one."

Nearby, Javix landed a final blow on John's chin, sending him down for the count. He nodded at Conrad, then all three of them turned to face Cyscope.

"Impressive," Cyscope said, clapping his hands. "But, amusing though all this has been, it is time to end it."

He moved with a speed near impossible for a body so old. In a flash he had Javix by the throat, and his soulblade gleamed at his belly.

"You will come with me, Hestar," Cyscope said, "or your friend here will suffer the consequences."

"Don't listen to him, kid," Javix said, struggling in Cyscope's grip. "If he kills this body I'll be released into spirit. I won't die."

"True," Cyscope said, "but while you are in that body, you can feel pain."

Cyscope touched the tip of his blade to Javix's left hip, and Javix cried out.

"Leave him alone!" Conrad shouted, rushing forward.

"Stay where you are, boy," Cyscope said. "I can hurt your friend in a thousand ways."

"Don't listen!" Javix said. "Get out of here . . . aagh!" he cried as Cyscope burned him again.

"What do we do?" Lysta asked Conrad, who shrugged.

"Beats me," he said. "We just went through this, remember?"

Conrad stared at Cyscope, and wondered what Hestar would do. Conrad was not particularly fond of Javix, and he suspected Hestar would have happily left the bounty hunter to his fate. True, Javix was working for Pakfrida, the alien who wanted to get Conrad safely off-planet. However, Conrad was sure Pakfrida's ship would find him with or without Javix's help.

Hestar would charge into battle and let Javix be damned. He would win, take what he wanted, and slash aside anyone who stood in his way. Maybe he'd surrender if his best friend Gennex was held hostage, but he was not. Time to light up his soulblade and fight.

Except, he didn't want to. Javix may have been a bit of a jerk, but everything he'd done had been to protect him. As Conrad thought about this, something else occurred to him.

He was not Hestar anymore. He may have been in his previous life, but he was different now. Hestar had lived his life, and now it was Conrad's turn. It was time to be Conrad.

The moment he thought this, the moment he decided who he was, the pain in his leg vanished forever.

"Let him go," Conrad said. "I'll give you what you want."

"Hestar, no!" Javix cried as Conrad walked toward him.

"My name," Conrad said, "is Conrad. You did your best, Javix, but it's over now."

"Indeed it is," Cyscope said. "Tell me what I want to know, Hestar . . ."

"Conrad!" he shouted. "My name is Conrad now. Try to keep up with the times."

"Very well, Conrad," Cyscope said. "Tell me where you've hidden the Shadow Matrix."

At the mention of the name, it all came back. A long time ago, long before Hestar had learned the powers in his soul, he had crash-landed on an asteroid in a sector close to galactic centre. The Magnus's mapping system told him the asteroid had once been part of a planet that had blown apart for reasons unknown.

Stranded there for a month or so to repair his ship, Hestar had come across a strange cave while searching for raw materials. It wasn't a natural cave—it looked as if it had been tunneled out. Inside was a chamber, sculpted from the rock into a kind of cathedral. It was huge, wide and round, and very dark. Hestar had felt chills that had nothing to do with his environment suit as he walked past the natural stone pillars that marked a path to the chamber's far end.

And at that end . . .

On a large stone dais . . .

Surrounded by sculpted rock demons . . .

(Hestar thought, at the time, that those demon sculptures might be worth something.)

. . . was a black, triangular crystal attached to a yard-long scepter.

"The Shadow Matrix," Conrad said. "I remember where I found it, but I don't remember where it is now."

"Look into my eyes," Cyscope ordered. "I will scan your soul."

"Conrad," Lysta said, taking his arm.

"I have to," Conrad told her, then he turned back to Cyscope. "Okay, let's do this."

Chapter Twenty

Cyscope, still clutching Javix, stared into Conrad's eyes and probed the depths of Hestar's soul, searching for his answers. He skipped past anything that wasn't relevant and homed in on his target, but when he arrived he found the path was blocked.

"It's blocked," Cyscope said. "Someone has put a memory block on you."

"So that's why I can't remember," Conrad said.

"No matter," Cyscope said, staring into his eyes again. "I am skilled in removing such things. The process will be quick, but excruciatingly painful."

"What?" Conrad said. "Hey, you didn't say anything about—"

"Silence!" Cyscope said, burning a spot on Javix's chest. "You will bear the pain, Conrad, or he will bear much worse."

"Okay, fine," Conrad said, steeling himself.

Cyscope focused, and Conrad felt daggers punching into his head. He wanted to scream, but he knew he had to take it for Javix's sake. The pain got worse, and he could actually feel something egg-like in his mind starting to crack.

"Almost there," Cyscope said. "Almost . . ."

"No you don't!" Knowlton yelled, charging into the intersection and throwing himself at Cyscope.

"Oof!" Cyscope cried as he, Javix and Knowlton fell to the ground in a mess of arms and legs.

The pain in his head ended instantly. Conrad recovered his senses and took action.

"Knowlton, Javix, get away from him," Conrad shouted as he rushed forward. He was delighted to see his best friend safe and sound, but the last thing he wanted was for Cyscope to take another hostage.

Javix got a foot under Knowlton and hefted him into Conrad's arms. He began to rise but Cyscope caught him, grabbing him with one arm. Conrad pushed Knowlton aside and ran forward, but Cyscope had his soulblade drawn once more.

"Come no closer, boy," Cyscope told Conrad, pointing his blade at him.

Javix grabbed Cyscope's blade arm and wrestled with him. Conrad considered his options, then lit his soulblade and struck.

"Sorry, Javix," Conrad said as the stunned Javix fell from Cyscope's grip.

"Cool," Knowlton said. "Just like in Episode 46."

Conrad attacked again, this time with Cyscope as his target. Cyscope blocked Conrad's blade and backed off. Conrad put himself between Cyscope and the comatose Javix.

"Damn you, boy," Cyscope roared. "Where is the Shadow Matrix?"

"You had your chance," Conrad said.

"So be it," Cyscope said, and sprang forward.

Cyscope and Conrad came together and clashed, and it was then that Conrad fully appreciated how much bigger the alien was. The body Cyscope had chosen was much stronger than he was, and had a longer reach. Cyscope took full advantage of this; he allowed Conrad to block his blade, then shoved forward mightily. Conrad fell on his back, and Cyscope laughed.

Enraged, Conrad leapt back up and threw his weapon forward. Cyscope blocked Conrad's soulblade thrusts with ease, then he drove a kick into his chest. Conrad flew backward and skidded along the pavement, and Knowlton and Lysta winced.

"Had enough?" Cyscope said with a chuckle as Conrad lay clutching his chest.

"Never," Conrad said, standing back up. Cyscope's kick had really hurt; he couldn't let him land another one.

Cyscope charged in, laying into Conrad with powerful lunges while staying well out of his adversary's range. Conrad deflected Cyscope's blows, keeping himself balanced and not allowing the larger alien to out-muscle him.

The tactic kept him on his feet, but it got him no closer to defeating Cyscope. Conrad's arms simply weren't long enough to reach past his opponent's defenses to land a hit.

Plus, Cyscope was really good. It was clear to Conrad that the alien was toying with him. As much skill as Hestar had, Cyscope seemed to have even more.

"Give it up, boy," Cyscope said, and Conrad barely got his soulblade up in time to save his left arm. "Surrender now, while you still have all your limbs."

Conrad gulped, realizing Cyscope wasn't planning to kill him. The alien still needed the information in Conrad's head, but his arms and legs were expendable. Conrad remembered how much losing his leg had hurt when he'd been Hestar, and he was in no hurry to go through that again.

The fear made him careless; Cyscope pushed his soulblade aside with his own, then elbowed Conrad in the side of the head. Conrad fell to the ground once more, reeling from the blow.

"You can never defeat me, boy," the alien said, standing over him.

"Don't listen to him, Conrad," Knowlton said. "You can take him."

"That's right," Conrad said, jumping back up. "I know I can take you. Because I did. Twelve years ago, just before . . ."

He stopped. This was the bit his mind wouldn't let him remember. Maybe it was another block, like the one protecting the Shadow Matrix's location. Whatever it was, it filled him with a queasy anxiety.

"Ah, yes, I do remember," Cyscope said. "The last time my Hunters and I came for you, on the Light Movement's base on Proxys. That wasn't long after you'd lost your leg."

"I still beat you," Conrad said. "And we stopped you from finding the Shadow Matrix."

"Of course you did," Cyscope said. "Because it was shortly after you killed me that Pakfrida killed you."

"What?" Conrad said.

And then he remembered.

The battle for Proxys had been huge. It had been devastating. The Light Movement had been crushed.

Hestar, with a fresh robotic leg replacing his lost limb, had his final battle with Cyscope while the base fell apart all around him. The battle had been long and tiring, and he hadn't been at all sure he would win.

But he won. At a critical moment Cyscope had been distracted, and Hestar had lopped his head off.

"Thanks for the help," Hestar had said to the approaching Pakfrida. "I thought he had me for sure."

"Cyscope wanted to take you alive," Pakfrida had said. "You have what he wants. And without the Light Movement to hide you . . ."

"Are things going that bad?"

"We are lost," Pakfrida had said. "They will take you, Hestar, and then the universe will fall to the power of evil."

"I can still escape," Hestar had said. "Where's Gennex? We'll take the Magnus and . . ."

"I'm sorry, Hestar," Pakfrida had said, and slid his soulblade into Hestar's chest. "Flee from here, my friend. I will come for you when we are ready."

Hestar had stared into Pakfrida's eyes a moment longer, then he'd collapsed to the floor, dead.

"I see you remember," Cyscope said. "It must have been devastating for you, to be killed by your mentor. Your soul flashed out of there faster than I could follow, but I've found you now."

"Yeah, and I'll take you down again," Conrad said. "I remember how I beat you the last time."

"Yes, Pakfrida distracted my attention," Cyscope said. "But that won't happen now. There is nothing that can possibly distract me from . . . what?"

The streetcorner filled with light. Cyscope looked up at the source, and Conrad leapt forward and struck. Cyscope crumpled to the street, stunned.

"Gotcha," Conrad said, and tried to think of a good line. "Um . . . I got it! How's that for déjà vu?"

"Um, Conrad," Knowlton said, pointing upward.

Conrad looked.

"Wow," he said.

A large, cigar-shaped UFO hung in the air above the city. It hovered vertically, tall as three skyscrapers, directly over the spot where Conrad stood. The light coming from all over the craft's golden exterior was bright enough to turn the night into day.

"There's something you don't see too often, huh?" Knowlton said, staring up at the ship.

"Wow," said Lysta, gazing up with them.

A green beam shone down from the ship, landing just in front of Conrad. He looked into the beam, remembered what it was, and knew what he had to do.

"Help me with Javix," he said. "We've got to get him into the beam."

"Why?" asked Lysta as she and Knowlton took hold of Javix's arms. "What is it?"

"It's a transport beam," Conrad said. "It'll take him up to the ship. And," he paused, taking hold of Javix's legs, "I'm going, too."

"Whoa! Really?" Knowlton said. "But you don't know where this ship is going."

"It's Pakfrida's ship, the Luminous," Conrad said. "He brought me aboard once, long ago. It will take me off Earth, which is good."

"No, it's not!" Knowlton said. "Con, you're my . . . my . . . well, who am I going to watch *Destiny* with?"

"I can't stay, Knowlton," Conrad said as he stepped into the beam. "Too many aliens know I'm here. More will come for me if I stay."

"Well, I'm coming too," Knowlton said, stepping into the beam with him. "After all, I'm an alien like you. Hey, so's Lysta. We're all aliens! We don't belong here."

"Speak for yourself," Lysta said, looking over Knowlton's shoulder at her mother, who had just arrived on the street corner with

Knowlton's parents. "I may have an alien soul, but this is my home. My mom . . . "

That was all she had time to say. The green beam covered all four of them, and plucked them from the surface of the Earth.

"Knowlton!" cried Knowlton's parents as they watched their son vanish into the ship.

"Lysta!" cried Lysta's mom, joining the Cabbages in watching the cigar-shaped ship rise up into the night sky. A second later, the ship sped away and vanished into space.

Epilogue

Cyscope awoke in the back seat of Javix's car. Eelt and Zepher sat up front, Quaz and Vellen beside him.

"What happened?" he asked as he returned to his senses. "Where is the quarry?"

"We failed," Eelt said. "I apologize, sir. We awoke too late to prevent Hestar and Gennex from escaping."

"Gennex?" Cyscope said. "That boy is not Gennex. He's someone else."

"Who is he?" Quaz asked.

"It is not important at present," Cyscope told her. "Keep driving. Our ship will arrive in a few standard hours, and we shall resume our hunt for He . . . for Conrad then."

"Okay," Lysta said. "Everyone heard me say I wasn't coming, right?"

If Conrad or Knowlton heard her, they didn't show it. The two boys stared around the chamber they found themselves in, awed and amazed beyond words. They should have been frightened—Lysta certainly was—but they were on board a starship and could not contain their excitement.

Javix, still unconscious, lay on the floor beside them.

"This is so cool!" Knowlton squeaked, staring all around them. The chamber was as wide as a city block and as tall as a small building, and the ceiling glowed green light down on them.

The ceiling was the only interesting feature, however. Aside from that, the chamber was nothing more than a big, empty room with a few crates stacked against one corner. The floor beneath them was a silvery metal, the kind of floor you'd expect to find in a UFO.

"It's a little like the cargo hold of the Destiny," Conrad said.

"Guys, now is not the time to talk about *Infinite Destiny*, okay?" said Lysta, even though she couldn't help looking around at the alien chamber, either. After all, she was a fan of *Infinite Destiny*, too.

"Any time is the time to talk about *Destiny*," Knowlton said as he stared upwards. "Hey, who are those guys?"

Lysta and Conrad's heads snapped up. If there were aliens to be seen, they didn't want to miss them.

"What guys?" Lysta asked.

And then she saw them, four beings descending from the ceiling. Lysta strained her eyes, trying to make out the details of their bodies. They looked bipedal and bulky, like professional wrestlers.

"I think they're robots," Knowlton said as the beings got closer. "What do you think, Conrad?"

"You just might be right," Conrad said, "for a change."

The beings were indeed robots, made of metal and circuits. Their heads had very distinct facial features, however, and when they landed, Conrad realized he knew one of them.

"Pakfrida," he said to the lead robot.

"Indeed," Pakfrida said. "Greetings, my friends, and welcome aboard the Luminous."

Conrad stared at the being who had both mentored and killed him in his previous incarnation, and felt his hands bunch into fists.

To Be Continued . . .

What would you like to read?

Llewellyn would love to know what kinds of books you are looking for but just can't seem to find. Witches and wizards, psychics, aliens, or just plain scary stuff—what do you want to read about? What types of books speak specifically to you? If you have ideas, suggestions, or comments, write Megan at:

megana@llewellyn.com

Llewellyn Publications
Attn: Megan, Acquisitions
2143 Wooddale Drive
Woodbury, Minnesota 55125-2989 USA
1-800-THE MOON (1-800-843-6666)
teen.llewellyn.com